William Ernest Henley

Life, Genius, Achievement

William Ernest Henley

Life, Genius, Achievement

ISBN/EAN: 9783337058029

Printed in Europe, USA, Canada, Australia, Japan

Cover: Foto ©Raphael Reischuk / pixelio.de

More available books at **www.hansebooks.com**

· PRICE 1/

' *Interesting, brilliant, full of original things.*'
THE TIMES.

BURNS
Life, Genius
Achievement
By W. E. HENLEY

WITH PORTRAIT

EDINBURGH: T. C. and E. C. JACK

LONDON: WHITTAKER AND CO

PATERNOSTER SQUARE, E.C.

1898

'THE CENTENARY BURNS'

Edited by W. E. HENLEY and T. F. HENDERSON

OPINIONS OF THE PRESS

THE TIMES.

This is, in many respects, infinitely the most thorough edition of Burns.

PALL MALL GAZETTE.

It is a rare satisfaction to be able to say that we possess at last the definitive, final edition of Burns. It has been a century and more in arriving; but it was well worth waiting for. Nearly seventy years since, Carlyle spoke of the brave mausoleum shining over the poet's dust, and of more than one splendid monument reared to Burns's fame. In the monumental kind, it may safely be asserted without qualification or reserve that nothing has ever equalled, nothing is ever likely to surpass, *The Centenary Burns*, as presented to us by Mr. Henley and Mr. Henderson. Judged as a book to behold and handle, Messrs. Constable have done their part as well as possible: thanks to them and Messrs. Jack, no external advantage is lacking. But excellent as is the material execution of this first volume, the interest of the edition lies in the treatment of the writer by his editors. From the moment that it was known that Mr. Henley and Mr. Henderson had undertaken to edit Burns, something of uncommon excellence was looked for at their hands; and it must be frankly admitted that in the result the most highly-wrought expectations are

a

realised. Henceforth, if any fresh edition of Burns be called for (and it may be feared that the present editors have left nothing for those who follow them), it is at least certain that an entirely new standard of editing the poet has been established. Mr. Henley and Mr. Henderson have produced a piece of work as admirable as insight, knowledge, sympathy, labour, and minute scholarship can make it. . . . Here Mr. Henley and Mr. Henderson have met and beaten the pedant on his own chosen ground. The distinction of the latest editors is that Burns is treated with the critical respect due to a genius and a classic.

SCOTSMAN.

From cover to cover this [the first] volume yields testimony of the care and the thought, the taste and the cost bestowed upon its production. . . . Of the scholarship and literary acumen displayed in the Notes, it is also not easy to speak in adequate terms of praise.

SCOTSMAN.

On the revision of the text and on the annotation of these songs the editors have spared themselves no labour, pains, and research ; and thus they go forth again to the world cleared of much of the dust which had in the course of a century settled upon and dimmed the fine gold of Burns, and also illuminated by the fresh light which the editors have been fortunate enough to throw upon the origin and descent of the *Museum* and *Scottish Airs* pieces, drawn from early and hitherto unpublished sources of information.

ATHENÆUM.

The book is a monument of industry, acuteness, and literary judgment, and its conclusions will satisfy most students who are acquainted with Scottish literature, being in the main confirmatory of what they have learnt to regard as the truth about the poetic genesis of Burns.

ATHENÆUM.

The magnificent 'Centenary Edition.' . . . The notes in general are everywhere scholarly and suggestive, adding occasionally a touch of the same interest and pleasure to the text, from which they are judiciously separated, as an introduction by the great Sir Walter —than which we can conceive no higher literary praise.

ATHENÆUM.

We have at length before us the concluding volume of *The Centenary Burns*. It is right to record that to the end the editors have maintained the standard of scholarship, the wealth of comparison, the painstaking fidelity of examination, with which they set forth on a congenial enterprise.

GLASGOW RECORD.

The completed *Centenary Burns* is now before the world. . . . And, speaking with these four handsome volumes before one, and fresh from the reading of that remarkable essay, no other verdict can be passed than that the serious Burns student is now in possession of the most original, the most virile, the most reasonable, and the most lucid edition of his poet which has appeared. And here is the proper place also to say that the publishers have produced the work worthily, that it is not less a delight to the eye than it is tonic and stimulant to the mind. The fourth volume, containing something like a dozen portraits of the poet, is a little gallery in itself.

ST. JAMES'S GAZETTE.

The Centenary Edition of Burns is completed by the publication of the fourth volume, with Mr. Henley's essay on the life, genius, and achievement of the Scottish national poet. It is a work on which all concerned may be congratulated. The editors are entitled justly to

pride themselves on having given a classic text, the
result of a careful collation of all the available versions ;
an explanation of the allusions and a history of each
piece ; a full glossary for southern readers ; and, in
spite of some rather violent reproaches from the patriots
who love Burns not wisely but too well, they have done
some service to literary history, even at the expense of
literary legend, in their minute inquiries into the details
of Burns's art and amours.

SATURDAY REVIEW.

The Notes, which are a mine of information on all
that concerns Burns, his friends, his loves, his dissipa-
tions, and his songs generally, leave nothing to be
desired.

SATURDAY REVIEW.

The careful investigations of Messrs. Henley and
Henderson prove, if they prove anything, that the
startling phrases and quaint turns of metre which we
have been in the habit of identifying with Burns are in
very large measure the property not of one man but of
the Doric race of Scottish peasantry in general. . . The
result of these investigations is to render the figure of
Burns less supernatural and, to those who are mere
fetish-worshippers of his fame, less convincing.   But
more reasonable admirers will feel that he is now brought
more into line with other poets, and, in being made more
explicable, rendered, if possible, more sympathetic.

SATURDAY REVIEW.

It is evident that much labour has been bestowed on
this collation, and the result is a work of real scholarship,
with the various readings given as fully as in the best
German edition of a Greek classic, based on the fullest
knowledge of the existing materials.

SATURDAY REVIEW.

The *Centenary Burns* is now concluded, and we may congratulate every one who is concerned with it on a highly satisfactory piece of work.

ACADEMY.

The industry displayed in unmasking forgeries, and investigating so far as possible the genuine sources of Burns's songs, can be dimly surmised to be extraordinary, though only those who have covered similar ground can estimate it aright.

ACADEMY.

Every scrap that Burns wrote has been weighed and sifted; his life has been viewed, piece by piece, as through a binocular glass; his productions judged as if never a line had been written about him before; the history and the local setting of his ' every several piece ' recorded ; his indebtedness to his forebears examined; the text elucidated with notes alive with vigour and personality; a glossary added which makes the Scots dialect easy as English to the Southron.

BIRMINGHAM POST.

The scholarship devoted to the text has been carried . into the notes, and everything that can throw a light on Burns and the production of his poems has been gleaned, sifted, and skilfully arranged. The terms of unmitigated eulogy are those which flow to the pen-point—superb, magnificent, superlative, matchless, etc.

FIFE HERALD.

It may, in a word, be said that this edition of Scotland's national bard is the most scholarly and exhaustive ever published. This distinction was long occupied by Mr. Scott Douglas's edition ; but it must now take a second place to that of Messrs. Henley and Henderson.

FIFE HERALD.

The work stands unrivalled. Only those who have studied its pages can have any idea of the painstaking research, the enormous labour, and the wide literary and poetic knowledge which the conjoined editors— Messrs. W. E. Henley and T. F. Henderson—have brought to bear on the task they have undertaken. Libraries, archives, and private collections in all parts of Scotland, and even of the world, have been ransacked in order to verify the text and to get up information as to the origin and history of Burns's poems and songs.

FIFE HERALD.

Not only is it an authentic embodiment of the poet's genius; it is a monument to the devotion, critical acumen, and scholarship of the editors. When it is remembered that 'more than half the verse of Burns was published posthumously, and that he was especially "unthrifty of his sweets," bestowing them upon all and sundry,' it is hardly necessary to say that of all our poets he required careful editing. Edition after edition of his works has been published by editors of more or less competency, generally less; but not till the Messrs. Jack induced Messrs. Henley and Henderson to essay the task can it be said that Burns has been adequately edited. You have only to dip into these admirably got-up pages, and to glance at the Notes, to see with what care and discrimination the laborious work has been executed.

DAILY CHRONICLE.

Some critics have written as though the industry of Messrs. Henley and Henderson in tracing the origin of Burns's lyrics tended to belittle him or endanger his reputation. Nothing could be further from the truth. The editors have, indeed, been far more successful than any of their predecessors in discovering and collating the material on which Burns worked. They have had access to many private collections of manuscripts, broadsides, chapbooks, etc., and they have especially utilised the Herd MSS. in the British Museum, which had escaped the notice of previous editors. The zeal and tact which they have brought to their task are beyond all praise, and the result is an important and permanent contribution to literary history. But in none of the records which have leaped to light is Burns for one moment shamed.

PUBLISHERS' CIRCULAR.

Messrs. Henley and Henderson are the most thorough, as they are among the very ablest, of the many editors and critics of Burns. Not an allusion is allowed to pass unexplained, nor is the most trivial piece of information bearing on Burns or his works omitted.

PUBLISHERS' CIRCULAR.

It is a triumph of technical skill, the printing by Messrs. Constable being beyond praise. The paper, too, is of the kind that endures, and Mr. William Hole seems to us to have fairly surpassed himself in the illustrations. But it is when we come to deal with the editorial portion that the excellence of this edition becomes clear. In bibliographical detail the work is complete : that is to say, it includes all the information regarding the various Burns publications, whether books, tracts, or broadsheets, known or obtainable at the present time. And that particular field has now probably been reaped to exhaustion. It is in the notes, however, that the editors' talent—we had almost said genius—for research is best displayed. Nor are the notes less remarkable for critical insight and condensation than for range and accuracy.

PUBLISHERS' CIRCULAR.

It is no conventional compliment to say that every lover of Burns owes a debt of gratitude to the editors and publishers of the 'Centenary Edition' of the poet's works now complete in four handsome volumes. The edition is, in fact, a model. Messrs. Jack have done it something more than justice in point of production, while the labour bestowed upon it by Messrs. Henley and Henderson has been simply prodigious. Not a scrap of Burns literature has been overlooked; nor a possible source of information neglected. The notes evince a thoroughness in the study of everything bearing upon Burns and his career which must make this the standard edition for all serious students of his poetry. Here, indeed, we have the whole history of Scottish song from its obscure beginnings to its glorious culmination in the immortal exciseman.

STANDARD.

Only students of Scottish life and character who have delved deeply for themselves in the racy vernacular speech of which *The Poetry of Robert Burns* forms the splendid climax, are in a position to appreciate the care and scholarship which Mr. Henley and Mr. Henderson have lavished on the hitherto confused and uncertain text of the Ayrshire poet.

GLASGOW MAIL.

If we were to single out what must ever give this edition its distinctive and enviable place in the front rank of the many so-called standard editions, we would instance the Bibliography. Never before has there been gathered such a mass of fact, anecdote, and literary criticism, illustrative of the songs and poems, and so admirably arranged as really to give fresh zest and point to many of the poet's choicest thoughts and most characteristic references in satire and song.

ST. JAMES'S GAZETTE.

The cause of truth is certainly advanced by the labours of Messrs. Henley and Henderson.

SPEAKER.

For our generation, at all events, it is the final *Burns*; nothing like it has hitherto been attempted.

SPEAKER.

Edited in a manner hitherto reserved for the classics of the ancient world.

SPEAKER.

What are the chief points of the work? First, we have the only correct text of Burns. You miss a familiar lection : you find it in a note with the reason for its rejection, and you have the sources of all the readings. Thus, various mss. of a poem exist ; these are described and classified as A, B, C, etc., and where the reading chosen differs the alternative one is given with an exact reference. Second, Burns's place as a lyrist has been exactly determined. It was well known to all who did more than read his text that he had borrowed from old Scots singers —he elaborately explains so himself— but then it was not known with certainty how much he had taken, or whence he had taken it. The past literature of Britain has been tracked with amazing industry, and we now can tell his sources and recognise him as one who came in the fulness of time to gather up the old Scots songs, pass them through the fire of his genius, and give them out again enormously enriched and embellished.

PERTHSHIRE ADVERTISER.

In taking leave of the editors of this great work we give them our hearty thanks for having produced the most accurate and complete edition of Burns that we now have the privilege of possessing.

BIRMINGHAM GAZETTE.

Messrs. W. E. Henley and T. F. Henderson are to be congratulated on the completion of *The Centenary*

Burns. To this work they have devoted themselves with unflagging enthusiasm, and the greatest praise one can possibly bestow is to say that they have realised the very high ideal with which the task was undertaken. We have now a Burns of surpassing excellence in every respect, and while congratulating the editors we must also pay the meed of praise that is due to Messrs. T. C. and E. C. Jack, the publishers, who have so ably supported Messrs. Henley and Henderson by providing their work with all that it lay in the power of the printer, the engraver, and the binder to bestow. Many poems have been published in this Centenary Edition for the first time—filched from oblivion by the patient research of the editors, who have reason to be deeply grateful for the ready courtesy with which the fortunate owners and custodians of Burns MSS. have volunteered information and assistance. But above all we value the work because it gives us practically the first text that is worthy of being described as classic.

LIVERPOOL POST.

The great *Centenary Burns* is finished, and four fair volumes, the mere handling whereof affords a delicious sensation, enshrine for days to come the treasures of the peasant that made himself, and ever must remain, of his country, *pars magna*. Few of our British singers, modern ones at any rate, have received such a tribute of minute yet luminous editing as Mr. Henley and Mr. Henderson have bestowed upon their author, and the best proof of their skill and care is the fact that, so far as we are aware, no infuriated Burnso-maniac has discovered an error in their comments or their readings through which to attack the structure of their daring and original criticism.

THE WORLD.

The etchings by Mr. William Hole, R.S.A., are fully worthy of an edition which in every department leaves the best of its predecessors hopelessly in the background.

BORDER ADVERTISER.

An edition of his works of which it may be said in the words of the song—'O but ye've been lang o' comin',' but which has been well worth waiting for. The material they have amassed has been of large bulk, but they have risen to the occasion, and displayed scholarship, taste, and literary skill (especially in connection with the notes) on which nothing but high commendation can be bestowed. These notes form a veritable mine of information, and to beat this work will be an impossible task. The publishers have bound it and otherwise done their part with great credit to themselves, and Dominie Sampson would have no hesitation in styling it 'prodigious.'

MORNING POST.

The publication of the fourth volume of the Centenary Edition of Burns marks the completion of a work of high literary value, and one that is probably destined to occupy a place among the classics as an abiding authority on the true text of the poet's verse. Indeed, the editors seem to have so thoroughly covered the field of research in collating Burns's published and unpublished poems that there is little temptation for any future commentator to attempt an amplification, either of the work that can reasonably be attributed to the Bard, or of the explanatory notes in which his allusions are made clear and the circumstances under which he wrote are recorded.

WESTMINSTER GAZETTE.

The Centenary Edition is a monument of industry.

IRISH TIMES.

Now we have the perfect *Burns* upon our shelves, which will everywhere prevail over spurious, inadequate, and incorrect editions, of which there have been too many.

NOTES AND QUERIES.

It now forms the most trustworthy and authoritative edition as regards text, and one of the handsomest as regards paper, typography, and illustrations.

MANCHESTER GUARDIAN.

There is no decline of worth in the scholarship of this fourth and last volume. This *Centenary Burns* is by much the most signal and well-aimed piece of labour that the celebration year (1896) of the poet's death has called out, and we have distinguished the value of each volume as it came. The care taken in collation of texts and in sifting of genuine from dubious work, the completeness of the biographies, which much exceed all prior collections of the kind, and the outward beauty of the books, need from us no further recognition.

WEEKLY SUN.

The past week has seen the publication of the fourth and concluding volume of the beautiful *Centenary Burns*. With the complete edition now before him the reader is in a position to judge of the value of this remarkable and monumental achievement. At the conclusion of a hundred years since Burns's death we have before us what must be regarded as the final and canonical edition of his works : any future editions can be only reprints, or at least founded upon this. Other great poets have found their editors perhaps after the lapse of many centuries. Shelley alone left a widow who was able to unite rare discrimination and literary taste in the task of bringing out a complete volume of her husband's poems. What Dindorf, using the labours of his predecessors, has done for the Greek tragedians, what Bentley has done for Horace, and Munroe for Lucretius, this Messrs. W. E. Henley and

T. F. Henderson have done for Scotland's poet. Together they have carried out their task, and together they will reap the glory of this great classic, which henceforth will be the authoritative *Burns* of the bookshelf and of the library.

NOTTS GUARDIAN.

With this volume the handsome Centenary Edition of Burns is completed. It may at once be said that the work is one of great merit, from whatever point of view considered. Endless time has been spent in searching out and examining almost every manuscript or paper bearing on the poet or his productions, and the notes are voluminous, carefully done, and bear the impress of authority, while the glossary and glossarial index have been prepared with infinite pains. No more complete and authoritative *Burns* is obtainable than this Centenary Edition, and the editors and publishers are to be complimented on the general excellence of their product.

NOTES AND QUERIES.

To the present generation this latest, handsomest, and most trustworthy edition of Burns will suffice. . . . In all typographical respects the volume is worthy of the man and the occasion.

NOTES AND QUERIES.

For Southron readers this edition remains incomparably the best.

SPECTATOR.

The bibliographical research exhibited in the notes suggests an amount of toil not readily to be estimated.

WORLD.

A work which places all lovers of Burns under a heavy obligation to every one concerned in its production.

'THE CENTENARY BURNS'

The LIMITED LIBRARY EDITION on hand-made paper having been sold out shortly after publication (and now selling at a premium), the following editions may now be had :—

LIBRARY EDITION, in four vols. demy octavo, square back, paper label, with Frontispiece Portrait to each vol., at 7s. 6d. the vol., nett.

ILLUSTRATED EDITION, in four vols. demy octavo, buckram gilt, gilt top, with twenty Original Etchings by WILLIAM HOLE, R.S.A., eleven Authentic Portraits in Photogravure, and various facsimilia of MSS., price 10s. 6d. the vol., nett. (Reprinted December 1897.)

Of this latter form there is a limited impression of ninety numbered large paper copies on Arnold's hand-made paper, with the etchings printed on Japanese vellum as proofs before letters and signed by the artist, copies of which are still to be had, price £1, 11s. 6d. the vol., nett.

LIFE, GENIUS
ACHIEVEMENT

BURNS

EDINBURGH
AND F. ...
...

BURNS

LIFE, GENIUS

ACHIEVEMENT

BY

W. E. HENLEY

Reprinted from 'The Centenary Burns'

EDINBURGH
T. C. AND E. C. JACK
LONDON: WHITTAKER AND CO
1898

ack—
Hockerre

ROBERT BURNS

(1759-1796)

In 1759 the Kirk of Scotland, though a less potent
and offensive tyranny than it had been in the good
old times, was still a tyranny, and was still offensive
and still potent enough to make life miserable, to
warp the characters of men and women, and to turn
the tempers and affections of many from the kindly,
natural way. True it is that Hutcheson (1694-1746)
had for some years taught, and taught with such
authority as an University chair can give, a set of
doctrines in absolute antagonism with the principles on which the Kirk of Scotland's rule was based,
and with the ambitions which the majority in the
Kirk of Scotland held in view. But these doctrines,
sane and invigorating as they were, had not reached
the general ; and in all departments of life among
the general the Kirk of Scotland was a paramount
influence, and, despite the intrusion of some generous
intelligences, was largely occupied with the work of
narrowing the minds, perverting the instincts, and
constraining the spiritual and social liberties of its
subjects. In 1759, however, there was secreted the
certainty of a revulsion against its ascendency ; for
that year saw the birth of the most popular poet,
and the most anti-clerical withal, that Scotland ever

bred. He came of the people on both sides; he had
a high courage, a proud heart, a daring mind, a
matchless gift of speech, an abundance of humour
and wit and fire; he was a poet in whom were quintessentialised the elements of the Vernacular Genius,
in whose work the effects and the traditions of the
Vernacular School, which had struggled back into
being in the Kirk's despite, were repeated with surpassing brilliancy; and in the matter of the Kirk
he did for the people a piece of service equal and
similar to that which was done on other lines and
in other spheres by Hutcheson and Hume and
Adam Smith. He was apostle and avenger as well
as maker. He did more than give Scotland songs to
sing and rhymes to read: he showed that laughter
and the joy of life need be no crimes, and that
freedom of thought and sentiment and action is
within the reach of him that will stretch forth his
hand to take it. He pushed his demonstration to
extremes; often his teaching has been grossly misread
and misapprehended; no doubt, too, he died of his
effort—and himself. But most men do as they must
—not as they will. It was Burns's destiny, as it
was Byron's in his turn, to be 'the passionate and
dauntless soldier of a forlorn hope'; and if he fell
in mid-assault, he found, despite the circumstances
of his passing, the best death man can find. He
had faults and failings not a few. But he was
ever a leader among men; and if the manner of
his leading were not seldom reckless, and he did
some mischief, and gave the Fool a great deal of
what passes for good Scripture for his folly, it will
be found in the long-run that he led for truth—

the truth which 'maketh free'; so that the Scotland
he loved so well, and took such pride in honouring,
could scarce have been the Scotland she is, had
he not been.

I

His father, William Burness (or Burnes), and his
mother, Agnes Brown, came both of yeoman stock:
native the one to Kincardineshire, the other to Ayrshire. William Burness began life as a gardener, and
was plying his trade in the service of one Fergusson,
the then Provost of Ayr, when, with a view to setting
up for himself, he took a lease of seven acres in the
parish of Alloway, with his own hands built a two-
roomed clay cottage—(still standing, but in use as
a Burns Museum),—and in the December of 1757
married Agnes Brown, his junior by eleven years.
She was red-haired, dark-eyed, square-browed, well-
made, and quick-tempered. He was swarthy and
thin; a man of strong sense, a very serious mind,
the most vigilant affections,[1] and a piety not even
the Calvinism in which he had been reared could
ever make brooding and inhumane. And in the
clay cottage to which he had taken his new-married
wife, Robert, the first of seven children, was born
to them on the 25th January 1759.

---

[1] In times of storm, he would seek out and stay with his
daughter, where she was herding in the fields, because he knew
that she was afraid of lightning; or, when it was fair, to teach
her the names of plants and flowers. He wrote a little
theological treatise for his children's guidance, too, and was,
it is plain, an exemplary father, and so complete a husband that
there is record of but a single unpleasantness between him and
Agnes his wife.

The Scots peasant lived hard, toiled incessantly, and fed so cheaply that even on high days and holidays his diet (as set forth in *The Blithesome Bridal*) consisted largely in preparations of meal and vegetables and what is technically known as 'offal.' But the Scots peasant was a creature of the Kirk; the noblest ambition of Knox[1] was an active influence in the Kirk; and the Parish Schools enabled the Kirk to provide its creatures with such teaching as it deemed desirable. William Burness was 'a very poor man' (R. B.). But he had the right tradition; he was a thinker and an observer; he read whatever he could get to read; he wrote English formally but with clarity;[2] and he did the very best he could for his children in the matter of education. Robert went to school at

---

[1] The Reformer had a vast deal more in common with Burns than with the 'sour John Knox' of Browning's ridiculous verses. He was the man of a crisis, and a desperate one; and he played his part in it like the stark and fearless opposite that he was. But he was a humourist, he loved his glass of wine, he abounded in humanity and intelligence, he married two wives, he was as well beloved as he was extremely hated and feared. He could not foresee what the collective stupidity of posterity would make of his teaching and example, nor how the theocracy at whose establishment he aimed would presently assert itself as largely a system of parochial inquisitions. The minister's man who had looked through *his* keyhole would have got short shrift from *him*; and in the Eighteenth Century he had as certainly stood with Burns against the Kirk of Scotland, as represented by Auld and Russell and the like, as in the Sixteenth he stood with Moray and the nobles against the Church of Rome, as figured in David Beaton and the 'twa infernal monstris, Pride and Avarice.'

[2] See the aforesaid treatise:—'*A Manual of Religious Belief, in a Dialogue between Father and Son,* compiled by William Burnes, farmer at Mount Oliphant, and transcribed, with grammatical corrections, by John Murdoch, teacher.'

six;[1] and in the May of the same year (1765) a lad of eighteen, one John Murdoch, was 'engaged by Mr. Burness and four of his neighbours to teach, and accordingly began to teach, the little school at Alloway': his 'five employers' undertaking to board him 'by turns, and to make up a certain salary at the end of the year,' in the event of his 'quarterly payments' not amounting to a specified sum. He was an intelligent pedagogue—(he had William Burness behind him)—especially in the matter of grammar and rhetoric; he trained his scholars to a full sense of the meaning and the value of words; he even made them 'turn verse into its natural prose order,' and 'substitute synonymous expressions for poetical words and . . . supply all the ellipses.'[2] One of his school-books was the Bible, another Masson's *Collection of Prose and Verse*, excerpted from Addison[3] and Steele and Dryden,

---

[1] 'I was a good deal noted at these years,' says the *Letter to Moore*, 'for a retentive memory, a stubborn, sturdy *something* in my disposition, and an enthusiastic *idiot*-piety. . . . In my infant and boyish days, too, I owed much to an old maid of my mother's, remarkable for her ignorance, credulity, and superstition,' who had, 'I suppose, the largest collection in the county of tales and songs concerning devils, ghosts, fairies, brownies, witches, warlocks, spunkies, kelpies, elf-candles, death-lights, wraiths, apparitions, cantraips, enchanted towers, giants, dragons, and other trumpery. This cultivated the latent seeds of Poesy,' etc.

[2] As Robert Louis Stevenson has remarked (*Some Aspects of Robert Burns*):—'We are surprised at the prose style of Robert ; that of Gilbert need surprise us no less.'

[3] 'The earliest thing of composition I recollect taking pleasure in, was *The Vision of Mirza*, and a hymn of Addison's beginning, "How are thy servants blessed, O Lord"' (R. B., *Letter to Moore*). 'The first two books,' he adds, 'I ever read in private, and which gave me more pleasure than any two books I ever read again, were the *Life of Hannibal* and the *History of Sir William*

from Thomson and Shenstone, Mallet and Henry
Mackenzie, with Gray's *Elegy*, scraps from Hume
and Robertson, and scenes from *Romeo and Juliet*,
Othello, and *Hamlet*. And one effect of his method
was that Robert, according to himself, ' was absolutely a critic in substantives, verbs, and participles,'
and, according to Gilbert, ' soon became remarkable
for the fluency and correctness of his expression,
and read the few books that came in his way with
much pleasure and improvement.' It is very characteristic of Murdoch that when, his school being
broken up, he came to take leave of William Burness
at Mount Oliphant, ' he brought us,' Gilbert says,
' a present and memorial of him, a small English
grammar and the tragedy of *Titus Andronicus*,' and
that ' by way of passing the evening ' he ' began to
read the play aloud.' Not less characteristic of all
concerned was the effect of his reading. His hearers
melted into tears at the tale of Lavinia's woes, and,
' in an agony of distress,' implored him to read no
more. Ever sensible and practical, William Burness
remarked that, as nobody wanted to hear the play,
Murdoch need not leave it. Robert, ever a sentimentalist and ever an indifferent Shakespearean,[1]

Wallace. Hannibal gave my young ideas such a turn that I used
to strut in raptures up and down after the recruiting-drum and
bag-pipe, and wish myself tall enough that I might be a soldier ;
while the story of Wallace poured a Scottish prejudice in my
veins which will boil along there (*sic*) till the floodgates of life
shut in eternal rest.'

[1] If we may judge him from his extant work. *Cf.* the absurd
line :—

'Here *Douglas* forms wild Shakespeare into plan.'

He cribs but once from Shakespeare, and the happiest among his

—'Robert replied that, if it was left, he would burn it.' And Murdoch, ever the literary guide, philosopher, and friend, was so much affected by his pupil's 'sensibility,' that 'he left *The School for Love* (translated, I think, from the French)' in Shakespeare's place.[1]

At this time Burns had but some two and a half years of Murdoch. William Burness liked and believed in the young fellow; for when, still urged by the desire to better his children's chance, he turned from gardening to cultivation on a larger scale, and took, at a £40 rental, the farm of Mount Oliphant, his two sons went on with Murdoch at Alloway, some two miles off. The school once broken up, however, Robert and his brother fell

---

few quotations is prefixed to one of the most felicitous—and therefore the least publishable—of his tributes to the Light-heeled Muse. 'Sing me a bawdy song,' he says with Sir John Falstaff, 'to make us merry.' And he adds this note,' in which he is Shakespearean once again :—'There is—there must be some truth in original sin. My violent propensity to b—dy convinces me of it. Lack a day ! If that species of composition be the special sin never-to-be-forgotten in this world nor in that which is to come, then I am the most offending soul alive. Mair for token,' *etc.* (R. B. to Cleghorn, 25th October 1793).

[1] There is no trace of any *School for Love*. It is therefore probable that what Gilbert meant was *The School for Lovers* : 'A Comedy. As it is acted at the Theatre Royal in Drury Lane. By William Whitehead, Esq. ; Poet Laureat. London : Printed for R. and J. Dodsley in Pall-Mall ; and Sold by J. Hinxman, in Pater-noster-row. MDCCLXII.' The first sentence of the author's *Advertisement* runs thus :—'The following Comedy is formed on a plan of Monsieur de Fontenelle's, never intended for the stage, and printed in the eighth volume of his works, under the title of *Le Testament.*' The names of the chief 'persons represented' are Sir John Dorilant, Modely, Belmour, Lady Beverley, Cælia, and Araminta : an unlikely lot, one would say, for an Ayrshire farmstead, even though it sheltered the youthful Burns.

into their father's hands, and, for divers reasons,
Gilbert says, 'we rarely saw any body but the
members of our own family,' so that 'my father
was for some time the only companion we had.'
It will scarce be argued now that this sole companionship was wholly good for a couple of lively
boys ; but it is beyond question that it was rather
good than bad.   For, 'he conversed on all subjects
with us familiarly, as if we had been men,' and,
further, 'was at great pains, as we accompanied him
in the labours of the farm, to lead the conversation
to such subjects as might tend to increase our knowledge or confirm our virtuous habits.'   Also, he got
his charges books — a *Geographical Grammar,* a
Physico and Astro-Theology, Stackhouse's *History of
the Bible,* Ray's *Wisdom of God in the Creation* ; and
these books Robert read ' with an avidity and industry scarcely to be equalled.'[1]   None, says
Gilbert, 'was so voluminous as to slacken his industry or so antiquated as to damp his research ':
with the result that he wasn't very far on in his

----

[1] Robert's list (*Letter to Moore*) includes Guthrie and Salmon's
Geographical Grammar ; *The Spectator* ; Pope ; 'some plays
of Shakespear' (acting editions? or odd volumes?) ; 'Tull and
Dickson on Agriculture'; *The Pantheon;* Locke *On the Human
Understanding;* Stackhouse; with 'Justice's *British Gardener,*
Boyle's *Lectures,* Allan Ramsay's *Works,* Dr. Taylor's *Scripture
Doctrine of Original Sin, A Select Collection of English Songs,*
and Harvey's *Meditations.'*   Later he knew Thomson, Shenstone,
Beattie, Goldsmith, Gray, Fergusson, Spenser even: with *The
Tea-Table Miscellany* and many another song-book, Adam
Smith's *Theory of the Moral Sentiments,* Reid's *Inquiry into the
Human Mind,* Bunyan, Boston (*The Fourfold State*), Shake-
speare, John Brown's *Self-Interpreting Bible,* and *The Wealth of
Nations,* which last he is found reading (at Ellisland) with a
sense of wonder that so much wit should be contained between

'teens ere he had 'a competent knowledge of ancient history,' with 'something of geography, astronomy and natural history.' Then, owing to the mistake of an uncle, who went to Ayr to buy a *Ready Reckoner or Tradesman's Sure Guide*, together with a *Complete Letter-Writer*, but came back with 'a collection of letters by the most eminent writers,' he was moved by 'a strong desire to excel in letter-writing.' At thirteen or fourteen he was sent ('week about' with Gilbert) to Dalrymple Parish School to better his handwriting; 'about this time' he fell in with *Pamela*, Fielding, Hume, Robertson, and the best of Smollett ; and 'about this time' Murdoch set up as a schoolmaster in Ayr, and 'sent us Pope's *Works* and some other poetry, the first that we had an opportunity of reading, excepting what is contained in the *English Collection* and in the volume of the *Edinburgh Magazine* for 1772.'[1] The summer after

---

the boards of a single book. One favourite novel was *Tristram Shandy*; another, the once renowned, now utterly forgotten *Man of Feeling*. At Ellisland, again, he is found ordering the works of divers dramatists—as Jonson, Wycherley, Molière—with a view to reading and writing for the stage. But you find no trace of them in his work; nor is there any evidence to show that he could ever have written a decent play, though there is plenty of proof that he could *not*. No doubt, *The Jolly Beggars* will be quoted against me here. But the essential interests of that masterpiece are character and description. Now, there go many more things to the making of a play than character, while, as for description, the less a play contains of that the better for the play.

[1] The *English Collection* I take to be Masson's aforesaid. At all events I can find no other. So far as verse is concerned, another exception was found in 'those *Excellent new Songs* that are hawked about the country in baskets or spread on stalls in the streets' (G. B.). They were probably as interesting to Robert as Pope's *Works* or the poetry in *The Edinburgh Magazine*. At

the writing-lessons at Dalrymple, Robert spent three weeks with Murdoch at Ayr, one over the English Grammar, the others over the rudiments of French.   The latter language he was presently able to read,[1] for the reason that Murdoch would go over to Mount Oliphant on half-holidays, partly for Robert's sake and partly for the pleasure of talking with Robert's father. Thus was Robert schooled; and 'tis plain that in one, and that an essential particular, he and his brother were exceptionally fortunate in their father and in the means he took to train them.[2]

In another respect—one of eminent importance—their luck was nothing like so good. Mount Oliphant was made up of 'the poorest land in Ayrshire'; William Burness had started it on a borrowed hundred; he was soon in straits; only by unremitting diligence and the strictest economy could he hope to make ends meet; and the burden of hard work lay heavy on the whole family—heavier, as I think, on the growing lads than on

---

any rate, his first essays in song were imitated from them, and he had the trick of them, when he listed, all his life long.

[1] Currie saw his Molière at Dumfries. There is no question but he would have got on excellent well with Argan and Jourdain and Pourceaugnac; but could he have found much to interest him in Arnolphe and Agnès, in Philinte and Alceste and Célimène? I doubt it. On the other hand, he would certainly have loved the *flon-flons* which Collé wrote for the Regent's private theatre; and I have always regretted that he read (1789) to no better purpose the La Fontaine of the *Contes*: a Scots parallel to which he was exactly fitted to achieve.

[2] Robert mastered, besides, the first six books of Euclid, and even dabbled a little in Latin now and then: reverting to his 'Rudiments' (says Gilbert) when he was crossed in love, or had tiffed with his sweetheart.

the made man and woman. 'For several years,' says Gilbert, 'butcher's meat was a stranger to the house.' Robert was his father's chief hand at fifteen —'for we kept no hired servant'—and could afterwards describe his life at this time as a combination of 'the cheerless gloom of a hermit with the unceasing toil of a galley-slave.' The mental wear was not less than the physical strain: for William Burness grew old and broken, and his family was seven strong, and of money there was as little as there seemed of hope. The wonder is, not that Robert afterwards broke *out* but, that Robert did not then break *down* : that he escaped with a lifelong tendency to vapours and melancholia, and at the time of trial itself with that 'dull headache' of an evening, which 'at a future period . . . was exchanged,' says Gilbert, 'for a palpitation of the heart and a threatening of fainting and suffocation in his bed in the night-time.' William Burness is indeed a pathetic figure ; but to me the Robert of Mount Oliphant is a figure more pathetic still. Acquired or not, stoicism was habitual with the father. With the son it was not so much as acquired ; for in that son was latent a world of appetites and forces and potentialities the reverse of stoical. And, even had this not been : if Robert hadn't proved a man of genius, with the temperament which genius sometimes entails : he must still have been the worse for the experience. He lived in circumstances of unwonted harshness and bitterness for a lad of his degree ; with a long misery of anticipation, he must endure a quite unnatural strain on forming muscle and on nerves and a brain yet immature ; he had perforce to face the

necessity of diverting an absolute example of the
artistic temperament to laborious and squalid ends,
and to assist in the repression of all those natural
instincts—of sport and reverie and companionship
—the fostering of which is for most boys, have they
genius or have they not, an essential process of
development; and the experience left him with
stooping shoulders and a heavy gait, an ineradicable
streak of sentimentalism, what he himself calls
'the horrors of a diseased nervous system,' and
that very practical exultation in the *joie de vivre*,
once it was known, which, while it is brilliantly
expressed in much published and unpublished verse
and prose, is nowhere, perhaps, so naïvely signified
as in a pleasant parenthesis addressed, years after
Mount Oliphant, to the highly respectable Thomson : — ' Nothing (*since a Highland wench in the
Cowgate once bore me three bastards at a birth*) has
surprised me more than,' *etc.*   The rest is not to
my purpose : which is to argue that, given Robert
Burns and the apprenticeship at Mount Oliphant,
a violent reaction was inevitable, and that one's
admiration for him is largely increased by the reflection that it came no sooner than it did.   William
Burness knew that it must come ; for, as he lay
dying, he confessed that it troubled him to think of
Robert's future.   This, to be sure, was not at Mount
Oliphant : when Robert had done no worse than
insist on going to a dancing-school : but years after,
at Lochlie, when Robert had begun to assert himself.
True it is that at Kirkoswald—a smuggling village,
whither he went, at seventeen, to study mensura-
tion, 'dialling,' and the like—he had learned, he says,

'to look unconcernedly on a large tavern bill and mix without fear in a drunken squabble.' True it is, too, that at Lochlie the visible reaction had set in. But, so far as is known, that reaction was merely formal ; and one may safely conjecture that, as boys are not in the habit of telling their fathers everything, William Burness knew little or nothing of those gallant hours at Kirkoswald. For all this, though, he seems to have discerned, however dimly and vaguely, some features of the prodigious creature he had helped into the world ; and that he should not have discerned them till thus late is of itself enough to show how stern and how effectual a discipline Mount Oliphant had proved.

II

The Mount Oliphant period lasted some twelve years, and was at its hardest for some time ere it reached its term. 'About 1775 my father's generous master died,'[1] says Robert ; and 'to clench the curse we fell into the hands of a factor, who sat for the picture[2] I have drawn of one in my tale of "Twa Dogs." . . . My father's spirit was soon irritated, but not easily broken. There was a free-

---

[1] This was that Fergusson (of Ayr) in whose service William Burness had been at the time of his marriage with Agnes Brown, and (apparently) for some years after it—in fact, till he took on Mount Oliphant. This he did on a hundred pounds borrowed from his old employer ; and one may conjecture that the legal proceedings which Robert thus resented were entailed upon Fergusson's agents by the work of winding up the estate.

[2] 'Sat for the picture I have drawn of one' is precise and definite enough. But surely the Factor verses in *The Twa Dogs*

dom in his lease in two years more, and to weather
these *we retrenched expenses*'—to the purpose and
with the effect denoted! Then came easier times.
In 1777 William Burness removed his family to
Lochlie, a hundred-and-thirty-acre farm, in Tarbolton Parish. 'The nature of the bargain,' Robert
wrote to Moore, 'was such as to throw a little ready
money in his hand in the commencement,' or 'the
affair would have been impracticable.' At this
place, he adds, 'for four years we lived comfortably';
and at this place his gay and adventurous spirit began to free itself, his admirable talent for talk to
find fit opportunities for exercise and display. ' The
reaction set in, as I have said, and he took life as
gallantly as his innocency might, wore the only
tied hair in the parish, was recognisable from afar
by his fillemot plaid, was made a ' Free and Accepted Mason,' [1] founded a Bachelors' Club,[2] and

_____

are less a picture than a record of proceedings, a note on the
genus Factor :—

> 'He'll stamp and threaten, curse and swear,
> He'll apprehend them, poind their gear,
> While they must stand, wi' aspect humble,
> An' hear it a', and fear and tremble.'

The statement is accurate enough, no doubt, but where is the
'picture'? Compare the effect of any one of Chaucer's Pilgrims,
or the sketches of Cæsar and Luath themselves, and the Factor as
individual is found utterly wanting.

[1] Burns was always an enthusiastic Mason. The Masonic idea
—whatever that be—went home to him; and in honour of the
Craft he wrote some of his poorest verses. One set, the 'Adieu,
Adieu,' *etc.*, of the Kilmarnock Volume, was popular outside
Scotland. At all events, I have seen a parody in a Belfast chap
which is set to the tune of *Burn's Farewell*.

[2] It was, in fact, part drinking-club and part debating-society.
But Rule X. of its constitution insisted that every member must

took to sweethearting with all his heart and soul
and strength. He had begun with a little harvester
at fifteen; and at Kirkoswald he had been enamoured of Peggy Thomson to the point of sleepless
nights. Now, says his brother Gilbert, 'he was
constantly the victim of some fair enslaver'—sometimes of two or three at a time; and 'the symptoms
of his passion were often such as nearly to equal
those of the celebrated Sappho,' so that 'the agita-
tion of his mind and body exceeded anything I
know in real life.' Such, too, was the quality of
what he himself was pleased to call 'un penchant
à (*sic*) l'adorable moitié du genre humain,' in combination with that 'particular jealousy' he had ' of
people that were richer than himself, or who had
more consequence in life,' that a plain face was
quite as good as a pretty one: especially and particularly if it belonged to a maid of a lower degree
than his own. To condescend upon one's women—
to some men that is an ideal. It was certainly the
ideal of Robert Burns. 'His love,' says Gilbert,
'rarely settled upon persons of this description'—
that is, persons ' who were richer than himself, or
who had more consequence in life.' He must still
be Jove—still stoop from Olympus to the plain.
Apparently he held it was an honour to be admired
by him; and when, a short while hence (1786), he
ventured to celebrate, in rather too realistic a strain,

have at least one love-affair on hand; and if potations were generally thin, and debates were often serious, there can be no question
that the talk ran on all manner of themes, and especially on that
one theme which men have ever found fruitful above all others.
The club was so great a success that an offshoot was founded, by
desire, on Robert's removal to Mossgiel.

the Lass of Ballochmyle, and was rebuffed for his
impertinence—(it was so felt in those unregenerate
days!)—he was, 'tis said, extremely mortified.   In
the meanwhile, his loves, whether pretty or plain,
were goddesses all; and the Sun was 'entering
Virgo, a month which is always a carnival in my
imagination' the whole year round ; and the wonder
is that he got off so little of it all in verse which
he thought too good for the fire.   Rhyme he did
(of course), and copiously : as at this stage every
coming male must rhyme, who has instinct enough
to 'couple but *love* and *dove.*'   But it was not till
the end of the Lochlie years that he began rhyming
to any purpose.   Indeed, the poverty of the Lochlie
years is scarce less 'wonderful past all whooping'
than the fecundity of certain memorable months at
Mauchline : especially if it be true, as Gilbert and
himself aver, that the Lochlie love - affairs were
'governed by the strictest rules of modesty and
virtue, from which he never deviated till his twenty-
third year.'[1]   For desire makes verses, and verses

---

[1] Saunders Tait, the Tarbolton poetaster, insists that, long
before Mossgiel, Burns and Sillar—'Davie, a Brother Poet'—
were the most incontinent youngsters in Tarbolton Parish ; and,
after asseverating, in terms as solemn as he can make them, that
in all Scotland

'There's none like you and Burns can tout
        The bawdy horn,'

goes on to particularise, and declares that, what with 'Moll and
Meg,

        Jean, Sue, and Lizzey, a' decoy't,
        There's sax wi' egg.'

Worse than all, he indites a 'poem,' a certain *B—ns in his
Infancy,* which begins thus :—

rather good than bad, as surely as fruition leaves verses, whether bad or good, unmade.

It was natural and honourable in a young man of this lusty and amatorious habit to look round for a wife and to cast about him for a better means of keeping one than farm-service would afford. In respect of the first he found a possibility in Ellison Begbie, a Galston farmer's daughter, at this time a domestic servant, on whom he wrote (they say) his 'Song of Similes,' and to whom he addressed some rather stately, not to say pedantic, documents in the form of love-letters. For the new line in life, he determined that it might, perhaps, be flax-dressing; so, at the midsummer of 1781 (having just before been sent about his business by, as he might himself have said, 'le doux objet de son attachement') he removed to Irvine, a little port on the Firth of Clyde, which was also a centre of the industry in which he hoped to excel. Here he established himself, on what terms is not known, with one Peacock, whom he afterwards took occa-

'Now I must trace his pedigree,
Because he made a song on me,
And let the world look and see,
    Just wi' my tongue,
How he and Clootie did agree
    When he was young':—

and of which I shall quote no more. But Robert and his brother are both explicit on this point; and, despite the easy morals of the class in which the Bard sought now and ever 'to crown his flame,' it must be held, I think, as proven that he was *déniaisé* by Richard Brown at Irvine and by Betty Paton at Lochlie.

This is the place to say that I owe my quotations from Saunders Tait to Dr. Grosart, who told me of the copy (pro-

sion to describe as 'a scoundrel of the first water, who made money by the mystery of Thieving';[1] here he saw something more of life and character and the world than he had seen at Mount Oliphant and Lochlie; here, at the year's end, he had a terrible attack of vapours (it lasted for months, he says, so that he shuddered to recall the time); here, above all, he formed a friendship with a certain Richard Brown. According to him, Brown being the son of a mechanic, had taken the eye of 'a great man in the neighbourhood,' and had received

---

bably unique) of that worthy's Poems and Songs: 'Printed for and Sold by the Author Only, 1796': in the Mitchell Library, Glasgow, and at the same time communicated transcripts which he had made from such numbers in it as referred to Burns. As my collaborator, Mr. T. F. Henderson, was then in Scotland, I asked him to look up Tait's volume. It was found at last, after a prolonged search; was duly sent to the Burns Exhibition; and in a while was pronounced 'a discovery.' Tait, who was pedlar, tailor, soldier in turn, had a ribald and scurrilous tongue, a certain rough cleverness, and a good enough command of the vernacular; so that his tirades against Burns—(he was one of the very few who dared to attack that satirist)—are still readable, apart from the interest which attaches to their theme. It is a pity that some Burns Club or Burns Society has not reprinted them in full, coarse as they are.

[1] Nobody knows what this may mean. It seems to be only Robert's lofty way of saying that Peacock swindled him. What follows is explicit (*Letter to Moore*):—'To finish the whole, while we were giving a welcome carousal to the New Year, our shop, by the drunken carelessness of my partner's wife, took fire, and burned to ashes, and I was left, like a true poet, not worth sixpence.' How much is here of fact, how much of resentment, who shall say? What is worth noting in it all is that Burns, despite his 'penchant à l'adorable,' etc., is first and last a peasant so far as 'l'adorable moitié' is concerned, and, for all his sentimentalism, can face facts about it with all the peasant's shrewdness and with all the peasant's cynicism.

'a genteel education, with a view to bettering his situation in life.' His patron had died, however, and he had had perforce to go for a sailor (he was afterwards captain of a West-Indiaman). He had known good luck and bad, he had seen the world, he had the morals of his calling, at the same time that 'his mind was fraught with courage, independ-ance, and magnanimity, and every noble, manly virtue'; and Burns, who 'loved him,' and 'admired him,' not only 'strove to imitate him' but also 'in some measure succeeded.' 'I had,' the pupil owns, 'the pride before'; but Brown 'taught it to flow in proper channels.' Withal, Brown 'was the only man I ever saw who was a greater fool than myself when Woman was the presiding star.' Brown, however, was a practical amorist; and he 'spoke of a certain fashionable failing with levity, which hither-to I had regarded with horror.' In fact, he was Mephisto to Burns's Faust;[1] and 'here,' says the Bard, 'his friendship did me a mischief, and the consequence was, that soon after I assumed the plough, I wrote the enclosed *Welcome.*' This enclosure (to Moore) was that half-humorous, half-defiant, and wholly delightful *Welcome to His Love-Begotten Daughter,*[2] through which the spirit of the

---

[1] Brown denied it. 'Illicit love!' quoth he. 'Levity of a sailor! When I first knew Burns he had nothing to learn in that respect.' It is a case of word against word; and I own that I prefer the Bard's.

[2] 'The same cheap self-satisfaction finds a yet uglier vent when he plumes himself on the scandal at the birth of his first bastard child.' Thus Stevenson. But Stevenson, as hath been said, had in him 'something of the Shorter Catechist'; and either he did not see, or he would not recognise, that Burns's

true Burns—the Burns of the good years: proud,
generous, whole-hearted, essentially natural and
humane—thrills from the first line to the last.
And we have to recall the all-important fact, that
Burns was first and last a peasant,[1] and first and
last a peasant in revolt against the Kirk, a peasant
resolute to be a buck, to forgive the really scandal-
ous contrast presented in those versions of the
affair—(versions done in the true buckish style:
the leer and the grin and the slang in full
blast)—which he has given in *The Fornicator*, the
Epistle to John Rankine, and—apparently—the
Reply to a Trimming Epistle from a Tailor. At
the same time we must clearly understand that we
recall all this for the sake of our precious selves,
and not in any way, nor on any account, for the
sake of Burns. He was absolutely of his station
and his time; the poor-living, lewd, grimy, free-
spoken, ribald, old Scots peasant-world [2] came to
a full, brilliant, even majestic close in his work;
and, if we would appreciate aright the environment
in which he wrote, and the audience to which such
writings were addressed, we must transliterate into
the Vernacular Brantôme and the *Dames Galantes*
and Tallemant and the *Historiettes*. As for reading

rejoicings in the fact of paternity were absolutely sincere throughout his life.

[1] Here and elsewhere the word is used, not opprobriously but,
literally. Burns was specifically a peasant, as Byron was specifically a peer, and as Shakespeare was specifically a man of the
burgess class.

[2] I do not, of course, forget its many solid and admirable
virtues; but its elements were mixed, and it was to the grosser
that the Burns of these and other rhymes appealed.

them in Victorian terms—Early-Victorian terms, or
Late—that way madness lies: madness, and a Burns
that by no process known to gods or men could
ever have existed save in the lubber-land of some
Pious Editor's dream.

At Lochlie, whither he seems to have returned
in the March of 1782, the studious years[1] and the
old comparative prosperity had come, or were
coming, to a close. There had been a quarrel between William Burness and his landlord, one M'Clure,
a merchant in Ayr; and this quarrel, being about
money, duly passed into the Courts. Its circumstances are obscure; but it is history that arbitra-
tion went against the tenant of Lochlie, that he
was ordered to 'quite possession,' that he was
strongly suspected of 'preparing himself accordingly
by dispossessing of his stock and crops,' and that
a certain 'application at present craving' resulted,
on shrieval authority, in the 'sequestration' of all
the Lochlie stock and plenishing and gear. Whatever the rights and wrongs of the affair, an end
came to it with the end of William Burness. By
this time his health was broken—he was far gone
in what Robert calls 'a phthisical consumption';
and he died in the February of the next year
(1784), when, as the same Robert romantically puts
it in his fine, magniloquent fashion, 'his all went
among the rapacious hell-hounds that growl in the
Kennel of Justice.'[2] The fact that Robert and

---

[1] It was parish gossip that, if you called on William Burness at
meal-time, you found the whole family with a book in one hand
and a horn spoon in the other.

[2] M'Clure's 'answers' and 'counter-answers,' together with the
sheriff's officer's account of the seizure at Lochlie, were published

Gilbert were able (Martinmas 1783), when their
father's affairs were 'drawing to a crisis,' to secure
another farm—Mossgiel—in Mauchline Parish, some
two or three miles off Lochlie, is enough to show
that neither errors nor crosses, neither sequestra-
tions nor lampoons, had impaired the family credit.

III

William Burness had paid his children wages during
his tenancy of Lochlie; and the elder four, by present-
ing themselves as his creditors for wages due, were
enabled to secure a certain amount of 'plenishing

---

in *The Glasgow Herald* early in the present year (1897). I need
scarce say that Saunders Tait produced a *Burns at Lochly*, in
which he fell on his enemy tooth and claw. His statements are
as specific as M'Clure's, and are substantially in agreement with
some of them, besides :—

'To Lochly ye came like a clerk,
And on your back was scarce a sark,
The dogs did at your buttocks bark,
But now ye 're bra',
Ye pouch't the rent, ye was sae stark,
Made payment sma'.'

In another stanza, 'M'Clure,' he says—

'Ye scarcely left a mite
To fill his horn.
You and the Lawyers gied him a skyte,
Sold a' his corn.'

In a third he appears to record the particulars of a single combat
between Robert and his father's landlord :—

'His ain gun at him he did cock,
An' never spared,
Wi't owre his heid came a clean knock
Maist killed the laird.'

And in the last of all, after bitterly reproaching Robert and the
whole Burns race with ingratitude :—

and gear' wherewith to make a start at Mossgiel. It
was a family venture, in whose success the Burnesses
were interested all and severally, and to which each
one looked for food and clothes and hire (the
brothers got a yearly fee of £7 apiece); and, as all
were well and thoroughly trained in farming work,
and had never lived other than sparely, it was
reasonable in them to believe that the enterprise
would prosper. That it did not begin by prospering
was no fault of Robert's. He made excellent re-
solutions, and, what was more to the purpose, he
kept them—for a time. He 'read farming books'
(thus he displays himself), he 'calculated crops,' he
'attended markets'; he worked hard in the fields,

> 'M'Clure he put you in a farm,
> And coft you coals your a—— to warm
>   And meal and maut. . . .
> He likewise did the mailin stock,
>   And built you barns':—

he sets forth explicitly this charge:—

> 'M'Clure's estate has ta'en the fever,
> And heal again it will be never,
> The vagabonds, they ca' you clever,
>   Ye're sic a sprite,
> To rive fra' him baith ga' and liver,
>   And baith the feet.'

The fact of the Laird's generosity is reaffirmed with emphasis in
A Compliment:—

> 'The horse, corn, pets, kail, kye, and ewes,
> Cheese, pease, beans, rye, wool, house and flours,
> Pots, pans, crans, tongs, bran-spits, and skewrs,
>   The milk and barm,
> Each thing they had was a' M'Clure's,
>   He stock'd the farm.' . . .

And with the remark that '*Five hundred pounds they were
behind*,' the undaunted Saunders brings his libel to a close.

he kept his body at least in temperance and sober-
ness, and, as for thrift, there is Gilbert's word for it,
that his expenses never exceeded his income of £7
a year. It availed him nothing. Gilbert is said to
have been rather a theorist than a sound practician ;
and Robert, though a skilled farmer, cared nothing
for business, and left him a free hand in the conduct
of affairs. Luck, too, was against them from the
first; and very soon the elder's genius was revealed
to him, and he had other than farmer's work to do.
' In spite of the Devil,' he writes, ' the world, and
the flesh, I believe I should have been a wise man ;
but the first year, from unfortunately buying in bad
seed, the second, from a late harvest, we lost half
of both our crops.' Naturally, ' this ' (and some other
things) ' overset all my wisdom, and I returned,
"like the dog to his vomit"—(be it remembered, it
is Robert Burns who speaks : not I)—"and the sow
that was washed, to her wallowing in the mire."'
That the confession, with its rather swaggering
allusion to the Armour business, was true, is plain.
But we do not need Burns's assurance to know that,
though he could do his work, and prided himself on
the straightness of his furrows, he was scarce cut
out for a successful farmer—except, it may be, in
certain special conditions. Endurance, patience,
diligence, a devout attention to one's own interest
and the land's, an indomitable constancy in labour
to certain ends and in thought on certain lines—
these are some of the qualities which make the hus-
bandman ; and, this being so, how should Mossgiel
have prospered under Rab the Ranter? His head
was full of other things than crops and cattle. He

was bursting with intelligence, ideas, the consciousness of capacity, the desire to take his place among
men ; and in Mauchline he found livelier friends [1]
and greater opportunities than he had found·else-
where. Being a Scot, he was instinctively a theo-
logian ; being himself, he was inevitably liberal-
minded ; born a peasant of genius, and therefore a
natural rebel, he could not choose but quarrel with
the Kirk—especially as her hand was heavy on his
friends and himself,—and it was as a Mauchline man
that the best of his anti-clerical work was done.[2]

[1] As his landlord, the lawyer Gavin Hamilton, to whom he
dedicated the Kilmarnock Volume, and the story of whose wrangle
with the Mauchline Kirk-Session (see Vol. i. pp. 147-152, 188,
378-9, etc.) is to some extent that of Burns's assault upon the
Kirk (see Vol. ii. *Holy Willie's Prayer*, pp. 25-30, and Notes,
pp. 320-324). Another was Robert Aiken, also a lawyer, by
whom he was 'read into fame,' to whom he dedicated *The
Cotter's Saturday Night*, and whom he celebrated in an Epitaph
(Vol. i. p. 188). Yet another was Richmond, the lawyer's clerk,
whose room he was afterwards to share in Edinburgh, and who
appears to be partly responsible for the preservation of *The Jolly
Beggars*. Again, there was the Bachelors' Club, on the model of
that he had founded at Tarbolton, for whose edification, and in
explanation of whose function, he appears to have written *The
Fornicator* and *The Court of Equity*. This last is Burns's idea
of what the proceedings of the Kirk-Session ought, in certain
cases, to have been. It is capital fun, but something too frank
and too particular for latter-day print.

[2] He was ever a theological liberal and a theological dis-
putant—a champion of Heterodoxy, in however mild a form,
whose disputations made him notorious, so that his name was
as a stumbling-block and an offence to the Orthodox. For
the series of attacks which he delivered against the Kirk—*The
Holy Fair*, the *Address to the Deil*, *The Twa Herds*, *The Ordination*, *Holy Willie*, *The Kirk's Alarm*, the Epistles *To the Unco
Guid* and *To John Goldie*—see Vols. i. and ii. (Text and Notes).
There is no record of an appearance on the stool with Paton ; but
the circumstances of this his initial difficulty appear to be set

Then, too, he was full of rhymes, and they must out
of him : his call had come, and he fell to obeying it
with unexampled diligence.   More than all, perhaps,
he had the temperament of the *viveur*—the man who
rejoices to live his life ; and his appetites had been
intensified, his gift of appreciation made abnormal
(so to say), by a boyhood 'and an adolescence of
singular hardship and quite exceptional continence.
It is too late in the world's history to apologise
for the primordial instinct; and to do so at any
time were sheer impertinence and unreasoning ingratitude.   To apologise in the case of a man who
so exulted in its manifestations and results, and
who so valiantly, not to say riotously, insisted on
the fact of that exultation, as Robert Burns, were
also a rank and frank absurdity.   On this point
he makes doubt impossible.   The 'white flower
of a blameless life' was never a button-hole for
him :[1] his utterances, published and unpublished,

forth in the *Epistle to Rankine* (i. 155) and the *Reply to a Trimming Epistle* (ii. 96), with the Notes thereto appended.   All
these read, considered, and digested, what interest remains in
Burns's quarrel with the Kirk consists in the fact that, being a
person naturally and invincibly opposed to the 'sour-featured
Whiggism' on which the Stuarts had wrecked themselves, Burns
was naturally and invincibly a Jacobite.   His Jacobitism was, he
said, ' by way of *vive la bagatelle.*' He told Ramsay of Auchtertyre
that he owed it to the plundering and unhousing (1715) of his grand-
father, who was gardener to Earl Marischal at Inverurie (*sic*).   But
it came to him mainly through Gavin Hamilton (who was Episco-
palian by descent) and his own resentment of clerical tyranny.

[1] It is true that he wrote thus 'To a Young Friend':—

> 'The sacred lowe o' weel-plac'd love,
>   Luxuriantly indulge it ;
> But never tempt th' illicit rove,
>   Tho' naething should divulge it:

are there to show that he would have disdained the presumption that it ever could have been. And it is from Mauchline, practically, that, his affair with Betty Paton over and done with, and, to anticipate a little, his affair with Jean Armour left hanging in the wind, he starts on his career as amorist at large.

And now for a little narrative. In the November of 1784 Elizabeth Paton bore him a daughter: 'the First Instance,' so he wrote above his *Welcome*, 'that entitled him to the Venerable Appellation of Father.' The mother is described as 'very plain-looking,' but of 'an exceedingly handsome figure'; 'rude and uncultivated to a great degree,' with a 'strong masculine understanding, and a thorough, though unwomanly, contempt for any sort of refinement'; withal, 'so active, honest, and independent a creature' that Mrs. Burns would have had Robert marry her, but 'both my aunts and Uncle Gilbert opposed it,' in the belief that 'the faults of her character would soon have disgusted him.' There had been no promise on his part; and though the

---

> I waive the quantum o' the sin,
> The hazard of concealing;
> But, och! it hardens a' within,
> And petrifies the feeling!'

But there is plenty to show that the writer was a great deal better at preaching than at practice. And he owns as much himself in his own epitaph :—

> 'Is there a man, whose judgment clear
> Can others teach the course to steer,
> Yet runs, himself, life's mad career
> Wild as the wave?—
> Here pause—and, thro' the starting tear,
> Survey this grave.'

reporter (his niece, Isabella Begg) has his own sister's warrant—(Mrs. Begg, by the way, was rather what her brother, in a mood of acute fraternal piety, might possibly have called 'a bletherin' b—tch')— for saying that ' woman never loved man with a more earnest devotion than that poor woman did him,' he in nowise sentimentalised about her. She is identified with none of his songs; and while there is a pleasant reference to her in the *Welcome*:—

    ''Thy mither's person, grace, and merit':—

she is recognisably the 'paitrick' of the *Epistle to Rankine*, she is certainly the heroine of *The Forni-cator*, she probably does duty in the *Reply to a Trimming Epistle*, none of which pieces shows the writer's 'penchant à l 'adorable,' *etc.*, to advantage. No doubt, they were addressed to men. No doubt, too, they were, first and last, satirical impeachments of the Kirk: impeachments tinctured with the pea-sant's scorn of certain existing circumstances, and done with all the vigour and the *furia* which one particular peasant—a peasant who could see through shams and was intolerant of them—could with both hands bestow. And that the women did not resent their share in such things is shown by the fact that such things got done. It was 'the tune of the time' —in the peasant-world at least. Still, as Diderot says somewhere or other:—' On aime celle à qui on le donne, on est aimé de celle à qui on le prend.' And one can't help regretting that there are few or none but derisive references to Betty Paton in her lover's work.

IV

Of vastly greater importance than his mistresses, at this or any period of his life, is the entity, which, with an odd little touch of Eighteenth Century formality, he loved to call his Muse. That entity was now beginning to take shape and substance as a factor in the sum of the world's happiness; and the coming of that other entity in whose existence he took so high a pride and so constant a delight—I mean 'the Bard'—was but a matter of time. Burns had been ever a rhymester; and Burns, who, as Stevenson observed, and as the Notes to these Volumes have shown, 'was always ready to borrow the hint of a design, as though he had some difficulty in commencing,' had begun by borrowing his style, as well as divers hints of designs, from stall-artists and neighbour-cuckoos. But, once emancipated, once a man, once practically assured of the primal concerns of life, once conscious that (after all) he might have the root of the matter in him, the merely local poet begins to waver and dislimn, and the Burns of *Poor Mailie* (written at Lochlie) and the *Epistle to Davie* reigns — intermittently, perhaps, but obviously—in his stead. It is all over with stall-artists and neighbour - cuckoos. Poor Fergusson's book [1]

---

[1] Robert Fergusson (1750-1774) was certainly a prime influence in Burns's poetical life. Nevertheless—or shall I say consequently?—he has had less than justice from the most of Burns's Editors. Yet in his way he was so remarkable a creature that there can be no question but in his death, at four-and-twenty, a great loss was inflicted on Scottish literature. He had intelligence and an eye, a right touch of humour, the gifts of invention

has fallen into his hands, and (as he says in his ridiculous way) has 'caused him to string anew his wildly-sounding rustic lyre with emulating vigour.' At last the hour of the Vernacular Muse has come; and he is hip to haunch with such adepts in her mystery as the Sempills, and Hamilton of Gilbertfield, and Allan Ramsay, and Robert Fergusson, and the innominates whose verses, decent or not, have lived in his ear since childhood : catching their tone and their sentiment; mastering their rhythms; copying their methods; considering their effects in the one true language of his mind.[1] He could write

---

and observation and style, together with a true feeling for country and city alike; and his work in the Vernacular (his English verse is rubbish), with its easy expressiveness, its vivid and unshrinking realism, and a merit in the matter of character and situation which makes it—not readable only, but—interesting as art, at the same time that it is valuable as history, is nothing less than memorable : especially in view of the miserable circumstances—(the poor lad was a starveling scrivener, and died, partly of drink, in the public madhouse)—in which it was done. Burns, who learned much from Fergusson, was an enthusiast in his regard for him ; bared his head and shed tears over 'the green mound and the scattered gowans' under which he found his exemplar lying in Canongate Churchyard; got leave from the managers to put up a headstone at his own cost there, and wrote an epitaph to be inscribed upon it, one line of which—

'No storied urn nor animated bust,'

is somehow to be read in Gray's *Elegy in a Country Churchyard.* Fergusson was as essentially an Edinburgh product—(the old Scots capital : gay, squalid, drunken, dirty, lettered, venerable : lives in his verses much as Burns knew it twelve years after his death)—as the late R. L. S. himself; and, while I write, old memories come back to me of the admiring terms : terms half-playful, half-affectionate : in which the later artist was wont to speak of his all but forgotten ancestor.

[1] I do not forget that Dugald Stewart noted the correctness of his speech and the success with which he avoided the use of

deliberate English, and, when he wanted to be not
so much sincere as impressive and 'fine,' he wrote
English deliberately, as the worse and weaker part
of his achievement remains to prove.   He could
even write English, as Jourdain talked prose, 'without knowing it'—as we know from *Scots Wha
Hae.*   He read Pope, Shenstone, Beattie, Goldsmith, Gray, and the rest, with so much enthusiasm
that one learned Editor has made an interesting
little list of pilferings from the works of these distinguished beings.   But, so far as I can see, he
might have lived and died an English-writing Scot,
and nobody been a thrill or a memory the better
for his work.   It is true that much of the *Saturday
Night* and the *Vision* and the *Mountain Daisy* is
written in English;[1] but one may take leave to

Scotticisms.   But in his day Scots was, not an accent but, a living
tongue; and he certainly could not have talked at Mauchline and
at Dumfries as he did in a more or less polite and Anglified
Edinburgh.

[1] He contrives a compromise, to admirable purpose, too, in
Tam o' Shanter: which is written partly in English and partly in
the Vernacular.   But (1) *Tam o' Shanter* is in a rhythmus classical
in Scotland since the time of Barbour's *Bruce*; (2) the English
parts of *Tam o' Shanter* are of no particular merit as *poetry*—that
is, 'the only words in the only order'; and (3) the best of *Tam
o' Shanter* is in the Vernacular alone.   Contrast, for instance,
the diabolical fire and movement and energy of these lines :—

> 'They reeled, they set, they cross'd, they cleekit,
> Till ilka carlin swat and reekit,
> And coost her duddies to the wark,
> And linket at it in her sark' :—

with another famous—perhaps too famous—passage :—

> 'But pleasures are like poppies spread :
> You seize the flower, its bloom is shed,' etc.

In the second the result is merely Hudibrastic.   In the first the

wonder if these pieces, with so much else of Burns's own, would have escaped the 'iniquity of Oblivion,' had they not chanced, to their good fortune, to be companioned with *Halloween*, and *Holy Willie*, and *The Farmer to His Auld Mare*, and a score of masterpieces besides, in which the Vernacular is carried to the highest level—in the matter of force and fire, and brilliancy of diction, and finality of effect, to name but these—it has ever reached in verse.[1] Let this be as it may : there can be no question that when Burns wrote English he wrote what, on his own confession, was practically a foreign

---

suggestion—of mingled fury and stink and motion and heat and immitigable ardour—could only have been conveyed by the Vernacular Burns.

[1] It was Wordsworth's misfortune that, being in revolt against Augustan ideals and a worn-out poetic slang, he fell in with Burns, and sought to make himself out of common English just such a vocabulary as Burns's own.   For he forgot that the Vernacular, in which his exemplar achieved such surprising and delectable results, had been a *literary* language for centuries when Burns began to work in it—that Burns, in fact, was handling with consummate skill a tool whose capacity had been long since proved by Ramsay and Fergusson and the greater men who went before them ; and, having no models to copy, and no verbal inspiration but his own to keep him straight, he came to immortal grief, not once but many times.   It is pretended, too, that in the matter of style Burns had a strong influence on Byron.   But had he ?   Byron praises Burns, of course ; but is there ever a trace of Burns the lyrist in the Byron songs ? Again, the Byron of *Childe Harold* and the tales was as it were a Babel in himself, and wrote Scott *plus* Coleridge *plus* Moore *plus* Beattie and Pope and the Augustan Age at large ; while the Byron of *Beppo* and the *Vision* and *Don Juan* approves himself the master of a style of such infernal brilliancy and variety, of such a capacity for ranging heaven-high and hell-deep, that it cannot without absurdity be referred to anything except the fact that he also was a born great writer.

tongue—a tongue in which he, no more than Fergusson or Ramsay, could express himself to any sufficing
purpose; but that, when he used the dialect which
he had babbled in babyhood, and spoken as boy and
youth and man—the tongue, too, in which the
chief exemplars and the ruling influences of his
poetical life had wrought—he at once revealed
himself for its greatest master since Dunbar.[1] More,
much more, than that: his bearings once found,
he marked his use of it by the discovery of a
quantity hitherto unknown in literature. Himself,
to wit: the amazing compound of style and sentiment with gaiety and sympathy, of wit and tender-

---

[1] For that is what it comes to in the end. He may seem to
have little to do with Catholic and Feudal Scotland, and as little
with the Scotland of the Early Reformation and the First Cove-
nant. Also, it is now impossible to say if he knew any more of
Scott and Dunbar and the older makers (Davie Lindsay and
Barbour excepted) than he found in *The Ever Green*, which Ramsay
garbled out of *The Bannatyne MS.*, if he were read in Pinker-
ton (1786), or if he got much more out of Gawain Douglas than
the verse which serves as a motto to *Tam o' Shanter*: though
a letter to Cleghorn shows that he certainly possessed a copy of
that poet before 1796. The Scotland he represents, and of which
his verses are the mirror, is the Scotland out of which the 'wild
Whigs' crushed the taste for everything but fornication and
theology and such expressions of derision and revolt as *Jenny*
M'Craw and *Errock Brae*: the Scotland whose literary beginnings
date, you'd fancy, not from Henryson, not from Dunbar and
Douglas and the Lyon King-at-Arms, but from Sempill of Beltrees
and the men who figure in the three issues of Watson's *Choice*
Collection. But Ramsay and his fellows were a revival—not a
new birth. The Vernacular School is one and indivisible. There
are breaks in the effect; but the tradition remains unbroken.
And Burns, for all his comparative modernity, descends directly
from, and is, in fact, the last of that noble line which begins with
Robert Henryson.

ness with radiant humour and an admirable sense of art, which is Robert Burns.

He could write ill, and was capable of fustian. But, excepting in his 'Epigrams' and 'Epitaphs' and in his imitations of poets whose methods he did not understand, he was nearly always a great writer, and he was generally (to say the least) incapable of fustian in the Vernacular. In essaying the effects of Pope and Shenstone and those other unfamiliars, he was like a man with a personal hand set to imitate a writing-master's copy: he made as good a shot as he could at it, but there was none of himself in the result. It was otherguess work when he took on the methods and the styles in which his countrymen had approved themselves: these he could compass so well that he could far surpass his exemplars technically, and could adequately express the individual Burns besides. The *Death and Dying Words of Poor Mailie* (written at Lochlie, and therefore very early work) trace back to Gilbertfield's *Bonnie Heck*; but the older piece is realistic in purpose and brutal in effect, while in the later—to say nothing of the farce in Hughoc—the whole philosophy of life of a decent mother - ewe is imagined with delightful humour, and set forth in terms so kindly in spirit and so apt in style, that the *Death and Dying Words* is counted one of the imperishables in English letters. Contrast, again, the *Elegy*, written some time after the *Death and Dying Words*, on this immortal beast, with its exemplars in Watson and Ramsay :—

'He was right nacky in his way,
   An' eydent baith be night and day ;

He wi' the lads his part could play
    When right sair fleed,
He gart them good bull-sillar pay ;
    But now he 's dead. . . .'

' Wha 'll jow Ale on my drouthy Tongue,
To cool the heat of Lights and Lung?
Wha 'll bid me, when the Kaile-bell 's rung,
    To Buird me speed ? . . .
Wha 'll set me by the Barrel-bung ?
    Since Sanny 's dead ? . . .'

He was good Company at Jeists,
And wanton when he came to Feasts ;
He scorn'd the Converse of great Beasts
    [F]or a Sheep's-head ;
He leugh at Stories about Ghaists—
    Blyth Willie 's dead ':—

and you shall find the difference still more glaring.
Cleverness apart—cleverness and the touch of life,
the element of realism—the Laments for Hab Simson
and Sanny Briggs, for John Cowper and Luckie
Wood and the Writer Lithgow,[1] are merely squalid
and cynical ; while in every line the *Elegy*, in despite
of realism and the humorous tone and intent

---

[1] All five, together with Ramsay's on Luckie Spence (an Edinburgh bawd) and *Last Words of a Wretched Miser*, should be
read for the sake of their likeness, and at the same time their
unlikeness, to not a little in Burns, and in illustration of the truth
that the Vernacular tradition was one of humorous, and even
brutal realism. I have cited R. L. S. in connexion with Fergusson.
He had a far higher esteem for that maker than he had for that
maker's ancestor, Allan Ramsay. Yet he quoted to me one day
a stanza from the *John Cowper*, a certain phrase in which—a
phrase obscenely significant of death—was, we presently agreed,
as good an example of 'the Squalid-Picturesque' as could be
found out of Villon.

(essential to the models and therefore inevitable
in the copy) is the work of a writer of genius, who
is also a generous human being.[1] Very early work,
again, are *Corn Rigs* and *Green Grow the Rashes* ; in
suggestion, inspiration, technical quality, both are
unalterably Scots ; and in both the effect of mastery
and completeness is of those that defy the touch
of Time. To compare these two and any two of
Burns's songs in English, or pseudo-English, is to
realise that the poet of these two should never
have ventured outside the pale of his supremacy.
English had ten thousand secrets which he knew
not, nor could ever have known, except imperfectly;
for he recked not of those innumerable traditions,
associations, connotations, surprises, as it were ambitions, which make up the romantic and the literary
life of words — even as he was penetrated and
possessed by the sense of any such elements as
may have existed in the Vernacular. Thus, if he
read Milton, it was largely, if not wholly, with a
view to getting himself up as a kind of Tarbolton
Satan. He was careless, so I must contend, of
Shakespeare. With such knowledge as he could
glean from song-books, he was altogether out of
touch with the Elizabethans and the Carolines.
Outside the Vernacular, in fact, he was a rather

---

[1] His suppression of such an old-fashioned touch in the first
draft as this one :—

'Now Robin greetan chows the hams
        Of Mailie dead' :—

is significant. It is quite in the vein of *Bonnie Heck*, as indeed
are the first four stanzas. But it would have ruined the *Elegy*
as the world has known it since 1786.

unlettered Eighteenth Century Englishman, and
the models which he must naturally prefer before
all others were academic, stilted, artificial, and
unexemplary to the highest point. It may be
that I read the verse of Burns, and all Scots
verse, with something of that feeling of 'precious-
ness' which everybody has, I take it, in reading a
language, or a dialect, not his own : the feeling
which blinds one to certain sorts of defect, and
gives one an uncritical capacity for appreciating
certain sorts of merit. However this be, I can certainly read my mother-tongue; and most Englishmen—with, I should imagine, many Scots—will
agree with me in the wish that Burns, for all the
brilliant compromise between Scots and English
which is devised and done in *Tam o' Shanter* and
elsewhere, had never pretended to a mastery which
assuredly he had not, nor in his conditions ever
could have had.

I have stressed this point because I wish to stress
another, and with a view to making clear, and to
setting in its proper perspective, the fact that,
genius apart, Burns was, no miracle but, a natural
development of circumstance and time. The fact
is patent enough to all but them that, for a superstition's sake, insist on ignoring history, and decline
to recognise the unchanging processes of natural
and social Law. Without the achievement of
Æschylus, there can be no such perfection as
Sophocles : just as, that perfection achieved, the
decline of Tragedy, as in Euripides, is but a matter
of time. But for the Middle Ages and the reaction
against the Middle Ages there could have been

no Ronsard, no Rabelais, no Montaigne in France. Had there been no Surrey and no Marlowe, no Chaucer and no Ovid (to name no more than these in a hundred influences), who shall take on himself to say the shape in which we now should be privileged to regard the greatest artist that ever expressed himself in speech? It is in all departments of human energy as in the eternal round of nature. There can be no birth where there is no preparation. The sower must take his seedsheet, and go afield into ground prepared for his ministrations; or there can be no harvest. The Poet springs from a compost of ideals and experiences and achievements, whose essences he absorbs and assimilates, and in whose absence he could not be the Poet. This is especially true of Burns. He was the last of a school. It culminated in him, because he had more genius, and genius of a finer, a rarer, and a more generous quality, than all his immediate ancestors put together. But he cannot fairly be said to have contributed anything to it except himself. He invented none of its forms; its spirit was not of his originating; its ideals and standards of perfection were discovered, and partly realised, by other men; and he had a certain timidity, as it were a *fainéantise*, in conception—a kind of unreadiness in initiative—which makes him more largely dependent upon his exemplars than any great poet has ever been. Not only does he take whatever the Vernacular School can give in such matters as tone, sentiment, method, diction, phrase; but also, he is content to run in debt to it for suggestions as

regards ideas and for models in style. Hamilton
of Gilbertfield and Allan Ramsay conventionalise
the Rhymed Epistle; and he accepts the convention as it left their hands, and produces epistles
in rhyme which are glorified Hamilton-Ramsay.
Fergusson writes *Caller Water*, and *Leith Races*,
and *The Farmer's Ingle*, and *Planestanes and Causey*,
and the *Ode to the Gowdspink*; and he follows
suit with *Scotch Drink*, and the *Saturday Night*,
and *The Holy Fair*, and *The Brigs of Ayr*, and
the *Mouse* and the *Mountain Daisy*. Sempill of
Beltrees starts a tradition with *The Piper of Kil-
barchan*; and his effect is plain in the elegies
on Tam Samson and Poor Mailie. Ramsay sees
a Vision, and tinkers old, indecent songs, and
writes comic tales in glib octo-syllabics; and instinctively and naturally Burns does all three.
It is as though some touch of rivalry were needed
to put him on his mettle:[1] as though, instead of
writing and caring for himself alone—(as Keats and
Byron did, and Shelley: new men all, and founders
of dynasties, not final expressions of sovranty)—to
be himself he must still be emulous of some one

---

[1] It was with '*emulating* vigour' that he strung his 'wildly-
sounding rustic lyre'; and he read Ramsay and Fergusson not
'for servile imitation' but 'to kindle at their flame.' Another
instance, or rather another suggestion, from himself, and I have
done. It 'exalted,' it 'enraptured' him 'to walk in the sheltered
side of a wood, or high plantation, in a cloudy winter day,' and
hear the wind roaring in the trees. Then was his 'best season for
devotion,' for then was his mind 'rapt up in a kind of enthusiasm to
Him who . . . "walks on the wings of the wind."' The 'rapture'
and the 'exaltation' are but dimly and vaguely reflected in his
Winter. But if some ancestor had tried to express a kindred
feeling, then had *Winter* been a masterpiece.

else. This is not written as a reproach: it is
stated as a fact. On the strength of that fact
one cannot choose but abate the old, fantastic
estimate of Burns's originality. But originality (to
which, by the way, he laid no claim) is but one
element in the intricately formed and subtly
ordered plexus, which is called genius; and I
do not know that we need think any the less
of Burns for that it is not predominant in him.
Original or not, he had the Vernacular and its
methods at his fingers' ends. He wrote the heroic
couplet (on the Dryden-Pope convention) clumsily,
and without the faintest idea of what it had been in
Marlowe's hands, without the dimmest foreshadow-
ing of what it was presently to be in Keats's; he had
no skill in what is called 'blank verse '—by which I
mean the metre in which Shakespeare triumphed, and
Milton after Shakespeare, and Thomson and Cowper,
each according to his lights, after Shakespeare and
Milton; he was a kind of hob-nailed Gray in his use
of choric strophes and in his apprehension of the
ode. But he entered into the possession of such
artful and difficult stanzas as that of Montgomerie's
Banks of Helicon and his own favourite sextain as
an heir upon the ownership of an estate which he
has known in all its details since he could know
anything. It was fortunate for him and for his
book, as it was fortunate for the world at large—as,
too, it was afterwards to be fortunate for Scots
song—that he was thus imitative in kind and thus
traditional in practice. He had the sole ear of the
Vernacular Muse; there was not a tool in her
budget of which he was not master; and he took

his place, the moment he moved for it, not so much, perhaps, by reason of his uncommon capacity [1] as, because he discovered himself to his public in the very terms—of diction, form, style, sentiment even — with which that public was familiar from of old, and in which it was waiting and longing to be addressed.

It was at Mossgiel that the enormous possibilities in Burns were revealed to Burns himself; and it was at Mossgiel that he did nearly all his best and strongest work. The revelation once made, he stayed not in his course, but wrote masterpiece after master-piece, with a rapidity, an assurance, a command of means, a brilliancy of effect, which make his achievement one of the most remarkable in English letters. To them that can rejoice in the Vernacular his very titles are enough to recall a little special world of variety and character and delight: the world, in fact, where you can take your choice among lyrical gems like *Corn Rigs* and *Green Grow the Rashes* and *Mary Morison* and masterpieces of satire like *Holy Willie* and the *Address to the Unco Guid*. To this time belong *The Jolly Beggars* and *Halloween* and *The Holy Fair*; to this time the *Louse* and the *Mouse*, the *Auld Mare* and the *Twa Dogs*; to this time,

---

[1] In the same way Byron sold four or five editions of the *English Bards*, because it was written on a convention which was as old as Bishop Hall, and had been used by every satirist from the time of that master down to Mathias and Gifford. If he had cast his *libellus* into the octaves of *Don Juan*, the strong presumption is that it would have fallen still-born from the press. Other cases in point are Blake, Wordsworth, Shelley, Keats, and Browning: the manner of each was new, and not all have reached the general yet.

Scotch Drink and the *Address to the Deil*, the *Earnest
Cry* and the *Mountain Daisy*, the *Epistles* to Smith
and Rankine and Sillar and Lapraik, the *Elegies* on
Tam Samson and the never-to-be-forgotten Mailie,
the *Reply* to a Tailor and the *Welcome* and the *Saturday Night*. In some, as *The Ordination, The Holy
Tulyie*, and, despite an unrivalled and inimitable
picture of drunkenness, *Hornbook* itself, with others
in a greater or less degree, the interest, once you
have appreciated the technical quality as it deserves,
is very largely local and particular.[1]   In others,
as the *Saturday Night* and *The Vision* (after the
first stanzas of description), it is also very largely
sentimental ; and in both these it is further
vitiated by the writer's 'falling to his English,'
to a purpose not exhilarating to the student of
Shakespeare and Milton and Herrick.   But all
this notwithstanding, and notwithstanding quite a
little crowd of careless rhymes, the level of excellence is one that none but the born great writer
can maintain.   Bold, graphic, variable, expressive,
packed with observations and ideas, the phrases go
ringing and glittering on through verse after verse,
through stave after stave, through poem after poem,
in a way that makes the reading of this peasant a

---

[1] There is a sense in which the most are local—are parochial even.
In *Holy Willie* itself the type is not merely the Scots Calvinistic
pharisee : it is a particular expression of that type ; the thing is a
local satire introducing the 'kail and potatoes' of a local scandal.
Take, too, *The Holy Fair* : the circumstances, the manners, the
characters, the experience—all are local.   Apply the test to
almost any—not forgetting the *Tam o' Shanter* which is the top
of Burns's achievement—and the result is the same.

peculiar pleasure for the student of style.[1] And
if, with an eye for words and effects in words, that
student have also the faculty of laughter, then are
his admiration and his pleasure multiplied ten-fold.
For the master-quality of Burns, the quality which
has gone, and will ever go, the furthest to make him
universally and perennially acceptable—acceptable
in Melbourne (say) a hundred years hence as in
Mauchline a hundred years syne—is humour. His
sentiment is sometimes strained, obvious, and
deliberate—as might be expected of the poet who
foundered two pocket-copies of that very silly
and disgusting book, *The Man of Feeling*; and it

---

[1] It is not, remember, for 'the love of lovely words,' not for
such perfections of human utterance as abound in Shakespeare:—
    'Gilding pale streams with heavenly alchemy':—
in Milton:—
    'Now to the moon in wavering morrice move':—
in Keats:—
    'And hides the green hill in an April shroud':—
in Herrick:—
    'Ye have been fresh and green,
    Ye have been filled with flowers,
    And ye the walks have been
    Where maids have spent their hours':—
that we revert to Burns. Felicities he has—felicities innumerable; but his forebears set themselves to be humorous, racy,
natural, and he could not choose but follow their lead. Th
Colloquial triumphs in his verse as nowhere outside the *Vision*
and *Don Juan*; but for Beauty we must go elsewhither. He has
all manner of qualities: wit, fancy, vision of a kind, nature, gaiety,
the richest humour, a sort of homespun verbal magic. But, if we
be in quest of Beauty, we must e'en ignore him, and 'fall to our
English': of whose secrets, as I've said, he never so much as
suspected the existence, and whose supreme capacities were sealed
from him until the end.

often rings a little false, as in much of the *Saturday Night.* But his humour—broad, rich, prevailing, now lascivious or gargantuan and now fanciful or jocose, now satirical and brutal and now instinct with sympathy, is ever irresistible. Holy Willie is much more vigorously alive in London, and Sydney, and Cape Town to-day than poor drunken old Will Fisher was in the Mauchline of 1785. That 'pagan full of pride,' the vigilant, tricksy, truculent, familiar, true-blue Devil lives ever in Burns's part pitying and fanciful, part humorous and controversial presentment; but he has long since faded out of his strongholds in the Kirk :—

> ' But fare-ye-weel, Auld Nickie-Ben,
>   O, wad ye tak' a thocht, an' men',
>   Ye aiblins micht—I dinna ken—
>   Still hae a stake !
>   I'm wae to think upon yon den,
>   Ev'n for your sake.'

Lockhart, ever the true Son of the Manse, was so misguided—so mansified, to coin a word—as to wish that Burns had written a *Holy Fair* in the spirit and to the purpose of *The Cotter's Saturday Night.* But the bright, distinguishing qualities of *The Holy Fair* are humour and experience and sincerity; the intent of the *Saturday Night* is idyllic and sentimental, as its effect is laboured and unreal; and I, for my part, would not give my *Holy Fair*, still less my *Halloween* or my *Jolly Beggars*—observed, selected, excellently reported—for a wilderness of *Saturday Nights.* It is not hard to understand that (given the *prestance* of its author) the *Saturday Night*

was doomed to popularity from the first :[1] being of
its essence sentimental and therefore pleasingly un-
true, and being, also of its essence, patriotic—an
assertion of the honour and the glory and the piety
of Scotland. But that any one with an eye for fact
and an ear for verse should prefer its tenuity of
inspiration and its poverty of rhythm and diction
before the sincere and abounding humour and the
notable mastery of means, before the plenitude of
life and the complete accord of design and effect,
by which *Halloween,* and *The Holy Fair,* and nine-
tenths of the early pieces in the Vernacular are
distinguished, appears inexplicable. In these Burns
is an artist and a poet : in the *Saturday Night* he
is neither one nor other.   In these, and in *Tam
o' Shanter,* the Scots School culminates : as English
Drama, with lyrical and elegiac English, culminates
in *Othello* and the *Sonnets,* in *Antony and Cleopatra*
and the *Adonis* and *The Rape of Lucrece* : more
gloriously far than the world would ever have
wagered on its beginnings. It is the most individual asset in the heritage bequeathed by 'the
Bard'; and still more, perhaps,[2] than the Songs,

---

[1] And such popularity ! 'Poosie Nansie's'—(thus writes a
friend, even as these sheets are passing through the press)—'or
rather a house on the site of Poosie Nansie's, is, as you know,
still a tavern. There is a large room (for parties) at the back.
And what, think you, is the poem that, printed and framed and
glazed, is hung in the place of honour on its walls? "*The Jolly
Beggars*—naturally?" Not a bit of it. *The Cotter's Saturday
Night*! Surrounded, too, by engravings depicting its choicest
moments and its most affecting scenes.'
[2] I say, 'perhaps,' because Burns, among the general at least,
is better sung than read. But if the Songs, his own and those
which are effects of a collaboration, be the more national, the

it stamps and keeps him the National Poet. The
world it pictures—the world of 'Scotch morals,
Scotch Religion, and Scotch drink'—may be ugly
or not (as refracted through his temperament,
it is *not*). Ugly or not, however, it was the world
of Burns; to paint it was part of his mission; it
lives for us in his pictures; and many such attempts
at reconstruction as *The Earthly Paradise* and *The
Idylls of the King* will 'fade far away, dissolve,' and
be quite forgotten, ere these pictures disfeature or
dislimn. He had the good sense to concern himself
with the life he knew. The way of realism[1] lay

Poems are the greater, and it is chiefly to the Poems that Burns
is indebted for his place in literature.

[1] It is claimed for him, with perfect truth, that he went straight
to Nature. But the Vernacular makers seldom did anything else.
An intense and abiding consciousness of the common circum-
stances of life was ever the distinguishing note of Scots Poetry.
It thrills through Henryson, through Dunbar and the Douglas of
certain 'Prologus' to *Eneados*, through Lindsay and Scott,
through the nameless lyrist of *Peeblis at the Play* and *Christ's
Kirk on the Green*, through much of *The Bannatyne MS.*, the
Sempill of the *Tulchene Bischope*, the Montgomerie of the
Flyting with Polwarth and of certain sonnets:—

'Raw reid herring reistit in the reik.'

It is even audible in the *Guid and Godlie Ballats*; and after the
silence it is heard anew in the verse which was made despite the
Kirk, and in the verse which proceeded from that verse—the
verse, that is, of Ramsay and Fergusson and Burns. This vivid
and curious interest in facts is, as I think, a characteristic of the
'perfervid ingyne.' Compare, for instance, Pitscottie and Knox
on the murder of Cardinal Beaton. The one is something naïve,
the other as it were Shakespearean; but in both the element
of particularity is vital to the complete effect. These are two
instances only; but I could easily give two hundred. (See *post*
p. 323, Note 1.) To return to Burns and his treatment of
weather (say) and landscape. His verse is full of realities:—

broad-beaten by his ancestors, and was natural to
his feet; he followed it with vision, with humour,
with 'inspiration and sympathy,' and with art;
and in the sequel he is found to have a place of his
own in the first flight of English poets after Milton,
Chaucer, Shakespeare.

V

I take it that Burns was not more multifarious in
his loves than most others in whom the primordial
instinct is of peculiar strength. But it was written
that English literature—the literature of Chaucer,
Shakespeare, Fielding—should be turned into a
kind of schoolgirls' playground; so that careful
Editors have done their best to make him even as
themselves, and to fit him with a suit of practical
and literary morals, which, if his own verse and
prose mean anything, he would have refused, with
all the contumely of which his 'Carrick lips' were

'When lyart leaves bestrow the yird,
  Or, wavering like the bauckie-bird,
    Bedim cauld Boreas' blast;
  When hailstanes drive wi' bitter skyte. . . .'
'The burn stealing under the lang, yellow broom. . . .'
'When, tumbling brown, the burn comes down. . . .'
'The speedy gleams the darkness swallowed. . . .'
'Yon murky cloud is foul with rain. . . .'
'November chill blaws loud wi' angry sugh':—
all exactly noted and vividly recorded (a very instructive instance
is the 'burnie' stanza in *Halloween*; for he had, they say, a
peculiar delight in running water). But for great, imaginative
impressions:—
'Those green-robed senators of mighty woods,
  Tall oaks branch-charmèd by the earnest stars':—
you turn to other books than his.

capable, to wear.   Nothing has exercised their in-
genuity, their talent for chronology, their capacity
for invention (even), so vigorously as the task of
squaring their theory of Burns with the story of
his marriage and the legend of his Highland Lassie.
Now is the moment to deal with both.

Elizabeth Paton's child was born in the November
of 1784.   In the April of that year, a few weeks
after the general settlement at Mossgiel, he made
the acquaintance of Armour the mason's daughter,
Jean.   She was a handsome, lively girl; the
acquaintance ripened into love on both sides; and
in the end, after what dates approve a prolonged
and serious courtship, Armour fell with child.
Her condition being discovered, Burns, after some
strong revulsions of feeling against—not Jean, I
hope, but—the estate of marriage, gave her what
he presently had every reason to call 'an unlucky
paper,' recognising her as his wife; and, had things
been allowed to drift in the usual way, the world
had lacked an unforgotten scandal and a great
deal of silly writing.   This, though, was not to be.
Old Armour—('a bit mason body, who used to
snuff a guid deal, and gey af'en tak' a bit dram ')
—is said to have 'hated' Burns: so that he would
'reyther hae seen the Deil himsel' comin' to the
hoose to coort his dochter than him.'   Thus a
contemporary of both Armour and Burns; and in
any case Armour knew Burns for a needy and reckless man, the father of one by-blow, a rebel at
odds with the Orthodox, of whom, in existing
circumstances, it would be vain to ask a comfortable living. ·So he first obliged Jean to give up

the ' unlucky paper,' with a view to unmaking any
engagement it might confirm,[1] and then sent her
to Paisley, to be out of her lover's way. In the
meanwhile Burns himself was in straits, and had
half-a-dozen designs in hand at once. Mossgiel
was a failure; he had resolved to deport himself to the West Indies; he had made up his
mind to print, and the Kilmarnock Edition was
setting, when Jean was sent into exile. Worst of
all, he seems to have been not very sure whether
he loved or not. When he knew that he and she
had not eluded the Inevitable, he wrote to James
Smith that 'against two things—staying at home
and owning her conjugally '—he was ' fixed as fate.'
'The first,' he says, ' by heaven I will not do!' Then,
in a burst of Don-Juanism—Don-Juanism of the
kind that protests too much to be real—'the last,
by hell I will never do.' Follows a gush of sentimentalism (to Smith), which is part nerves and part
an attempt—as the run on the g's and the w's shows
—at literature :—' A good God bless you, and make
you happy, up to the warmest weeping wish of parting friendship.' And this is succeeded by a message
to the poor, pregnant creature, of whom, but two
lines before, he has sworn ' by hell ' that he will
never make her honest :—' If you see Jean, tell her

---

[1] I take it that the paper was 'unlucky,' because it became a
weapon in old Armour's hands, and was the means of inflicting on
the writer the worst and the most painful experience of his life.
At the same time there seems to be no doubt that it made Jean
Mrs. Burns, so that, consciously or not, Auld (who probably had
a strong objection to the marriage) was guilty of an illegal act in
certifying Burns a bachelor. Burns, in fact, was completely
justified in his anger with the Kirk and in the scorn with which
he visited the tyranny of her ministers.

I will meet her, so help me God in my hour of
need.' This scrap is undated, but it must have
been written before 17th February 1786, when he
wrote thus to Richmond:—'I am extremely happy
with Smith; he is the only friend I have *now* in
Mauchline.' Well, he *does* meet Jean; and, his better
nature getting the upper hand, the 'unlucky paper'
is written. Then on the 20th March he writes
thus to Muir:—'I intend to have a gill between us
or a mutchkin stoup,' for the reason that it 'will
be *a great comfort and consolation*':—which seems to
show that Jean has repudiated him some time between the two letters. Before the 2nd April, on
which day the Kirk-Session takes cognisance of the
matter, Jean has gone to Paisley; the 'unlucky
paper' is cancelled (apparently about the 14th
April, the names were cut out with a penknife);
so that Don Juan finds himself *planté-là*, and being
not really Don Juan—(as what sentimentalist could
be?)—he does not affect Don Juan any more. The
prey has turned upon the hunter; the deserter
becomes the deserted, the privilege of repudiation,
'by hell' or otherwise, has passed to the other
side. The man's pride, inordinate for a peasant,
is cut to the quick; and his unrivalled capacity
for 'battering himself into an affection' or a mood
has a really notable opportunity for display. In
love before, he is ten times more in love than ever;
he feels his loss to desperation; he becomes the
disappointed lover—even the true-souled, generous,
adoring victim of a jilt:—

'A jillet brak his heart at last
        That's owre the sea.'

In effect, his position was sufficiently distracting.
He had made oath that he would *not* marry Jean;
then he had practically married her; then he found
that nobody wanted her married to him—that, on
the contrary, he was the most absolute 'detrimental'
in all Ayrshire; when, of course, the marriage became the one thing that made his life worth living.
He tried to persuade old Armour to think better of
his resolve; and, failing, ran 'nine parts and nine
tenths out of ten stark staring mad.' Also he
wrote the *Lament*, in which he told his sorrows to
the moon[1] (duly addressing that satellite as 'O
thou pale Orb'), and took her publicly into his
confidence, in the beautiful language of Eighteenth
Century English Poetry, and painted what is in the
circumstances a really creditable picture of the
effects upon a simple Bard of 'a faithless woman's
broken vow.' Further, he produced *Despondency* in
the same elegant lingo; and, in *Despondency*, having
called for 'the closing tomb,' and pleasingly praised
'the Solitary's lot,'—

> 'Who, all-forgetting, all-forgot
>   Within his humble cell—
> The cavern, wild with tangling roots—
> Sits o'er his newly gathered fruits,
>   Beside his crystal well!' *etc.*—

he addressed himself to Youth and Infancy in these
affecting terms :—

---

[1] Is it worth noting that, later, when he comes to sing of
Mary Campbell, his confidant is no longer the Moon but the
Morning Star?

'O enviable early days,
  When dancing thoughtless Pleasure's maze,
  To care, to guilt unknown !
  How ill exchang'd for riper times,
  To feel the follies or the crimes
    Of others, or my own !
Ye tiny elves that guiltless sport,
  Like linnets in the bush,
Ye little know the ills ye court,
  When manhood is your wish !
    The losses, the crosses
      That active man engage ;
    The fears all, the tears all
      Of dim declining Age !' [1]

Moreover, he took occasion to refer to Jean (to
David Brice ; 12th June 1786) as 'poor, ill-advised,
ungrateful Armour'; vowed that he could 'have
no nearer idea of the place of eternal punishment'
than 'what I have felt in my own breast on her

---

[1] I cannot attach any great importance to these exercises in
Poetic English. Burns wrote to a very different purpose when
he wrote from his heart and in his native tongue :—

    'Had we never loved sae kindly . . .'
    'Of a' the airts the wind can blaw
      I dearly like the west' :—

and so on, and so on. Still, there can be no doubt that they
mean something. At any rate they are designed to be impressive
and 'fine'; and probably the Bard believed in them to the extent
to which he was satisfied with his achievement in what must certainly have seemed to him real poetry. None of your Vernacular
(that is), but downright, solid, unmistakable English Verse : verse
which might stand beside the works of Beattie and Shenstone and
Thomson and the 'elegantly melting Gray.' That life departed
them long since is plain. But it is just as plain that they meant
something to Burns, for (apparently) he took much pains with
them, saw not their humorous aspect, and included them in his
first (Kilmarnock) Volume.

account'; and finally confessed himself to this purpose:—' I have tried often to forget her: I have run
into all kinds of dissipation and riot . . . to drive her
out of my head, but all in vain.' Long before this,
however—as early, it would seem, as some time in
March—his ' maddening passions, roused to tenfold
fury,' having done all sorts of dreadful things, and
then 'sunk into a lurid calm,' he had 'subsided into
the time-settled sorrow of the sable widower,' and
had lifted his 'grief-worn eye to look for—another
wife.' In other words, he had pined for female
society, and had embarked upon those famous love-
passages with Highland Mary.

Little that is positive is known of Mary Campbell
except that she once possessed a copy of the
Scriptures (now very piously preserved at Ayr), and
that she is the subject of a fantasy, in bronze,
at Dunoon. But to consider her story is, almost
inevitably, to be forced back upon one of two
conclusions:—either (1) she was something of a
lightskirts; or (2) she is a kind of Scottish Mrs.
Harris. The theory in general acceptance—what
is called the Episode Theory—is that she was 'an
innocent and gentle Highland nursery-maid' (thus,
after Chambers, R. L. S.) 'in the service of a neigh-
bouring family' (Gavin Hamilton's); that she con-
soled Burns—*mais pour le bon motif*—for Jean's de-
sertion; that they agreed to marry; that, on her
departure for the West to prepare for the event,
' Ayr, gurgling, kissed his pebbled shore,' and they
exchanged vows and Bibles; and that she died, of a
malignant fever, some few months after her return to
Greenock. Another identifies her (on Richmond's

authority) with a serving-maid in Mauchline, who
was the mistress of a Montgomerie, and had withal
such a hold upon Burns that for a brief while he was
crazy to make her his wife ; and some have thought
that this may be the Mary Campbell who, according
to the Dundonald Session Records, fathered a child
on one John Hay. This last hypothesis is, of course,
most hateful to the puzzle-headed puritans who cannot, or will not, believe, despite the fact that the
world has always teemed with Antonies, each of
them mad for his peculiar Cleopatra, that Burns,
particularly in his present straits, might very well
have been enamoured of a gay girl to the point of
marriage.   So, for the consolation of these, there
has been devised a third, according to which her
name was either Mary Campbell or something unknown ; but, whatever she was called, she was so
far and away the purest and sweetest of her sex
—the one 'white rose,' in fact, which grew up
among 'the passion flowers' of the Bard's career
—that she must, had she married him, have entirely 'rectified' his character, and have trans-
formed him into a pattern Kirk-of-Scotland puritan
of the puritans.   On the other hand, it has become obvious to some whole-hearted devotees of
the Marian Ideal that a 'young person' of this sort
could scarce have been of so coming a habit as
to skip with alacrity into Jean's old shoes, and—
shutting her innocent eyes to the fact that Burns,
a man notoriously at war with the Kirk and the
seducer of two unmarried women, was at the same
time at his wits' end for cash—consent to cast in
her lot with his at a moment's notice and with

never a sign from the family she was to enter. If
she could do that, plainly she could not, except on
strong positive testimony, be made to do duty as a
white rose among passion-flowers; or if, on some
unknown and inenarrable hypothesis, she could,
then, says one of the devout, 'the conduct of Burns
was that of a scoundrel.' This is absurd! So of
late (1896-97) there has come into being a wish
to believe that either Mary Campbell preceded
Armour in the Bard's affections, or the Highland
Lassie never existed at all, but was a creature of
Burns's brain : an ideal of womanhood to which his
thought ascended from the mire of this world—(the
world of Ellisland, and Jean, and the children, and
the songs in Johnson's *Museum*)—as Dante's to his
Beatrice of dream. Given Burns's own habit and
the habit of the Scots peasant woman, there is
still no earthly reason for rejecting the Episode
Theory—even were rejection possible—however
seriously it reflect upon the morals of the parties concerned. But it is fair to add that the subject is both
complicated and obscure. Burns's own references
to his Highland Lassie are deliberately insignificant
and vague : for once in his life he was reticent. His
statement that she went home to prepare for their
marriage is heavily discounted by the fact that he did
not introduce her to his family as his betrothed, in
nowise prepared for marriage on his own account,
never dreamed, except in sporadic copies of verse,
of taking her to the West Indies, and was all the
while so desperately enamoured of Jean that not
by any amount of self-indulgence could he rid his
breast of her : by the fact, too, that, if his thought

went back to the Highland Lassie in after years, his
report of the journey is strongly tinctured with
remorse.[1]   Currie's statement is that 'the banks of
Ayr formed the scene of youthful passions . . . the
history of which it would be improper to reveal,' etc.
Gilbert Burns, after noting that Nanie Fleming's
charms were 'sexual'—'which indeed was the
characteristic of the greater part of his (Robert's)
mistresses'—is careful, perhaps with an eye on the
heroine of Thou Ling'ring Star, to record the statement that Robert, at least, 'was no platonic lover,
whatever he might pretend or suppose of himself to
the contrary.'   There is Richmond's statement, as
reported by Train.   There is the Mary Campbell of
the Dundonald Register.   There is the certainty
that relations there were between Burns and a Mary
Campbell.   There is the strong probability that Mary
Campbell and the Highland Lassie were one and
the same person.   There is Burns's own witness to
the circumstance that they met and parted under
extremely suspicious conditions.   That, really, is
all.   Yet, on the strength of a romantic impulse on
the part of Robert Chambers, the heroine-in-chief
of Burns's story is not the loyal and patient soul
whom he appreciated as the fittest to be his wife
he'd ever met: not the Jean who endured his
affronts, and mothered his children (her own and
another's), and took the rough and the smooth,

---

[1] He sent *Thou Ling'ring Star* to Mrs. Dunlop in a letter
dated 8th November 1789.   In acknowledging it, the lady noted
its remorseful cast, and hoped it didn't set forth a personal experience.   There is nothing to show that he gave her any particulars, or essayed to disabuse her of the idea that remorse there
well might be.

the best and the worst of life with him, and wore his name for well-nigh forty years after his death as her sole title to regard. On the contrary, that heroine-in-chief is a girl of whom scarce anything definite is known, while what may be reasonably suspected of her, though natural and feminine enough, is so displeasing to some fanatics, that, for Burns's sake (not hers) they would like to mythologise her out of being; or, at the least, to make her as arrant an impossibility as the tame, proper, figmentary Burns, the coinage of their own tame, proper brains, which they have done their best to substitute for the lewd, amazing peasant of genius,[1] the inspired faun, whose voice has gone ringing through the courts of Time these hundred years and more, and is far louder and far clearer now than when it first broke on the ear of man.

Stevenson was an acute and delicate critic at many points; but he wrote like a novelist—like Thackeray, say, of Fielding and Sterne—when he wrote of Armour as a 'facile and empty-headed girl,' and insisted, still possessed by Chambers's vain imaginings, that she was first and last in love with another man. In truth the facility was on the other side. In 1784 Burns is willing to marry Betty Paton, and writes thus to Thomas Orr:—'I am very glad Peggy [Thomson] is off my hand, as I am at present embarrassed enough without her.' In 1785 he is courting Jean Armour, and very early in 1786 Jean is in the family way, and 'by hell' she shall never be his wife. But some time in March

---

[1] 'Peculiarly like nobody else' (R. B. to Arnot, April 1786).

Jean is sent to Paisley; and the 'maddening
passions,' *etc.*, set to work; and he can no more 'se
consoler de son départ' than Calypso could for that
of Ulysses. So in a hand's turn he becomes the
stricken deer, and, as we have seen, protests (to the
Moon) that to marry Jean, and wear 'The promised
father's tender name' are his sole ambitions. As
Jean does not return, however, he seeks (and finds)
such comfort as he may in exchanging vows and
Bibles and what Chamfort called 'fantaisies' with
Mary Campbell. On the 12th-13th May he writes
The Court of Equity—a task the strangest conceivable for a lover, whether rejoicing or distraught.
On the 14th 'Ayr gurgling kisses his pebbled
shore,' and 'The flowers spring wanton to be
pressed,' and Highland Mary leaves for the West
to make these famous preparations. On the 15th
May he dates (at least) the *Epistle to a Young
Friend* :—

  ' The sacred lowe o' weel-placed love
   Luxuriantly indulge it,' *etc.* :—

and, as for some time past, he is still the gallant,
howbeit in jest, of Betty Miller: till on the 9th June
'poor ill-advised Armour' returns to Mauchline;
and on the 12th he writes that 'for all her part in a
certain black affair' he 'still loves her to distraction,'
and, with a view to forgetting her has 'run into all
kinds of dissipation and riot . . . but in vain.' On
the 28th June he appears before 'the Poacher
Court,' acknowledges paternity, and is 'promised a
certificate as a single man': on condition that he
do penance before the congregation on three suc-
cessive Sundays. On the 9th July, the occasion

of his first appearance, he has 'a foolish hankering
fondness' for Jean, but, calling on her and being
put to the door, he remarks that she does not 'show
that penitencé that might have been expected'; so,
on the 22nd, he executes a deed by which he
makes over all his property to the 'wee image of
his bonie Betty,' to the exclusion of whatever
might come of his affair with the recusant.   Then,
on the 30th (old Armour having, meanwhile, got a
warrant against him, and sent him into hiding[1]), he
adjures Richmond—(who, he knows, will 'pour an
execration' on Jean's head)—to 'spare the poor,
ill-advised girl for my sake'; and on the 14th
August he calls on Heaven to 'bless the Sex,' for
that 'I feel there is still happiness for me among
them.'   Against this panorama of tumult and
variety and adventure, enlarged in Edinburgh, and
enriched at Ellisland and in Dumfries, there are to
set the years of simple abnegation, magnanimity,
and devotion with which the 'facile and empty-
headed girl' repaid the husband of her choice.
The conclusion is obvious.   The Novelist turned
Critic is still the Novelist.   Consciously or not, he
develops preferences, for, consciously or not, he
must still create.[2]   Stevenson's preferences were

---

[1] No doubt he retired on information sent by Jean.

[2] Thus Stevenson, who himself liked 'dressing a part' (so to
speak), was persuaded that Burns did likewise, and accepted bodily
that absurd, fantastic story (told by two Englishmen), in which
the Bard, in a fox-skin cap and an enormous coat, and girt with
a Highland broadsword, is seen angling from a Nithside rock.
Jean denied it, and said that Robert (who hated field-sports, as
we know) never angled in his life.   But the Novelist was roused;
and all that was ignored.

with Rab Mossgiel. And the result was a grave—
but not, I hope, a lasting—injustice to an excellent
and very womanly woman and a model wife.[1]

As to Highland Mary, one of two conclusions:
(1) Either she was a paragon; or (2) she was not.
In the first case, her story has yet to be written,
and written on evidence that is positive and irre-
futable. In the second, the bronze at Dunoon
bears abiding witness to the existence (at a certain
time) of what can only be described as a national
delusion.

VI

By this time the end of Mauchline, and of much
besides, was nearer than Burns knew. Probably sent
to press in the May of 1786, the Kilmarnock Volume
was published at the end of July.[2] Most of, if not

---

[1] On the 3rd September Jean lay in of twins. They were
presently taken by their respective grandmothers, to whom, I
doubt not, they gave great joy: as in that and other stages of
society the appearance of the third generation, whether its right to
exist be legal or not, does always. Burns announced the event
as only Burns could, by sending *Nature's Law*:—

> ' Kind Nature's care had given him share
> Large of the flaming current,' *etc.*:—

to Gavin Hamilton; a ' God bless the little dears'; with a snatch
of indecent song, to Richmond, and a really heartfelt and affecting bit of prose on the subject of paternity to Robert Muir.

[2] One effect of its publication was to secure him the friendship
of Mrs. Dunlop (ii. 352-3). It is evident from this lady's letters
that her interest in him could scarce have been warmer had he
been her son. She prized his correspondence as beyond rubies,
and as a rule he was slower to reply than she (once, being hurt
by his silence, she told him she wouldn't write again till he asked

all, the numbers contained in it were probably familiar to the countryside. Some had certainly been received with 'a roar of applause'; Burns, who was not the man to hide his light under a bushel (his temperament was too radiant and too vigorous for that), was given to multiplying his verses in MS. copies for friends; he had been 'read into fame' by Aiken the lawyer: so that *Poems, Chiefly in the Scottish Dialect* was, in a sense, as 'well advertised' as book could be. Its triumph was not less instant than well-deserved:[1] the first issue, six hundred copies strong, was exhausted in a month ('tis said that not one could be spared for Mossgiel). But Burns himself, according to himself, and he was ever punctiliously exact and scrupulous on the score of money, was but £20 in

---

her, and, failing to draw him, within a week she is found begging his pardon for her petulance). She made him many gifts— apparently in money and in kind—gifts at New Year and other times, and accepted gifts from him (once he sent her a keg of old brandy). Her influence made over for decency, and it may well have been on her remonstrances, which were strong, that he finally resolved to remove some of the coarser phrases in his earlier editions. Her last (extant) letter is dated 11th January 1795. For some unexplained reasons she ceased from writing several months before the January of 1796. It may have been that she heard of him as often in drink, or that she was told of the affair at Woodley Park. In any case she esteemed him so highly, and admired him so lavishly, that 'tis quite impossible to believe the breach in the correspondence due to any fault of hers.

[1] 'Old and young,' says Heron, 'high and low, grave and gay, learned or ignorant, all were alike delighted, agitated, transported. I was at that time resident in Galloway, contiguous to Ayrshire: and I can well remember, how that even the plough-boys and maid-servants would have gladly bestowed the wages which they earned the most hardly, and which they wanted to purchase necessary clothing, if they might but secure the works of Burns.'

pocket by it; the Kilmarnock printer declined to
strike off a second impression, with additions, unless
he got the price of the paper (£27) in advance; and
for some time it seemed that there was nothing but
Jamaica for the writer, Local Bard and Local Hero
though he were: so that he looked to have sailed in
mid-August, and again on the 1st September, and
at some indeterminate date had ' conveyed his chest
thus far on the road to Greenock,' and written that
solemn and moving song—far and away the best, I
think, and the sincerest thing he left in English
—*The Gloomy Night is Gathering Fast.* It was to be
the 'last effort' of his 'Muse in Caledonia.' But,
for one or another reason, his departure was ever
deferred; and, though on the 30th October (some
ten days, it is surmised, after the death of Mary
Campbell), he was still writing that, 'ance to the
Indies he was wonted,' he'd certainly contrive to
'mak' the best o' life Wi' some sweet elf,' on the
18th November, 'I am thinking for my Edinburgh
expedition on Monday or Tuesday come s'ennight.'
In effect, an 'Edinburgh expedition' was natural
and inevitable. Ballantine of Ayr is said to have
suggested the idea of such an adventure; Gilbert
and the family are said to have applauded it. But
as early as the 4th September the excellent Blacklock—(in 'a letter to a friend of mine which over-
threw all my schemes')—had called—'for the sake
of the young man'—for a second edition, 'more
numerous than the former': inasmuch as 'it appears
certain that its intrinsic merit, and the exertions of
the author's friends, might give it a more universal
circulation than anything of the kind which has

been published within my memory.' Thus Blacklock ; and the 'friend of mine,' which was Lawrie,
the minister of Loudoun, had communicated Blacklock's letter to the person most concerned in
Blacklock's suggestion. Bold, proud, intelligent *au
possible*, strongly possessed too (so he says, and so I
believe) by the genius of paternity, Burns the Man,
who had a very becoming opinion of Burns the
Bard, and could fairly appreciate that worthy's
merits, must certainly have seen that in Edinburgh
he had many chances of succeeding at the very
point where the Kilmarnock printer failed him.
I do not doubt, either, that he was tired of being
the Local Poet, the Local Satirist, the Local Wit,
the Local Lothario (even), and eager to essay
himself on another and a vaster stage than Mauchline ; for, if he hadn't been thus tired and thus
eager, he wouldn't have been Robert Burns. The
fighting spirit, the genius of emulation, is so strong
in us all that a man of temperament and brains
must assert himself, and get accepted at his own
(or another) valuation, exactly as a cock must
crow. And I love to believe that Burns, being
immitigably of this metal, entered upon his adventure—(27th November: on a borrowed nag, with
not much money, a letter of introduction to Dalrymple of Orangefield, and a visiting list consisting
entirely in Dugald Stewart and Richmond the
lawyer's clerk)—with the joyous heart and the stiff
neck of one who knows himself a man among men,
and whose chief ambition is to 'drink delight of
battle with his peers'—if he can find them.

He reached the capital on the 28th November,

and was hospitably entertained by Richmond—to
the extent, indeed, of a bedfellow's share in the
clerk's one little room in Baxter's Place, Lawn-
market.   Through Dalrymple of Orangefield he got
access to Lord Glencairn and others : among them
Harry Erskine, Dean of Faculty, and that curious,
irascible, pompous ass, the Earl of Buchan, and
Creech the publisher, who had been Glencairn's
tutor, and who advertised the Edinburgh Edition
on the 14th December.   He was everywhere received as he merited, and he made such admirable
use of his vogue that, five days before Creech's
advertisement was printed, he could tell his friend
and patron, Gavin Hamilton, that he was rapidly
qualifying for the position of Tenth Worthy and
Eighth Wise Man of the World.   He saw everybody
worth seeing, and talked with everybody worth talking to ; he was made welcome by 'heavenly Burnett'
and her frolic Grace of Gordon, and welcome by
the ribald, scholarly, hard-drinking wits and jinkers
of the Crochallan Fencibles, for whose use and
edification he made the unique and precious collection now called *The Merry Muses of Caledonia*; he
moved and bore himself as easily at Dugald Stewart's
as in Baxter's Place, in Creech's shop, with Henry
Mackenzie and Gregory and Blair, as at that extraordinary meeting of the St Andrew's Lodge, where,
at the Grand Master's bidding, the Brethren assem-
bled drank the health of 'Caledonia and Caledonia's
Bard—Brother Burns': a toast received with 'multiplied honours and repeated acclamations.'   To look
at, 'he was like a farmer dressed to dine with the
laird'; his manners were 'rustic, not clownish'; he

had 'a sort of dignified plainness and simplicity.'
Then, 'his address to females was always extremely
deferential, and always'—this on the authority of
the Duchess of Gordon—'with a turn to the pathetic
or humorous, which engaged their attention particularly.'   For the rest, 'I never saw a man in company
with his superiors in station and information more
perfectly free from either the reality or the affectation of embarrassment.'   Thus, long afterwards, Sir
Walter, who noted also, boy as he was, 'the strong
expression of sense and shrewdness in all his linea-
ments,' and who, long afterwards, had never seen
such an eye as Burns's 'in a human head, though
I have seen the most distinguished men'—
(Byron among them; and Byron's eye was one of
Byron's points)—'of my time.'   It is not wonderful, perhaps, that Burns, with his abounding
temperament, his puissant charm, his potency in
talk, his rare gifts of eye and voice,[1] should have
strongly affected Edinburgh Society, brilliant in its
elements and distinguished in its effect as it was.
There has been no Burns since Burns; or history
would pretty certainly have repeated itself.   What
is really wonderful is the way in which Burns kept
his head in Edinburgh Society, and stood prepared
for the inevitable reaction.   Through all the 'thick,
strong, stupefying incense smoke' (and there was
certainly a very great deal of it), he held a steady
eye upon his future.   He saw most clearly that the

---

[1] Thus Maria Riddell:—'His voice alone could improve upon
the magic of his eye.   Sonorous, replete with the finest modula-
tions,' etc.   It will be remembered that children used to speak
of Byron as 'the gentleman with the beautiful voice.

life of a nine-days' wonder is at most nine days,
and that now was his time or never. But if he expected preferment, he was neither extravagantly
elated in anticipation, nor unduly depressed by disappointment; and, for all his self-consciousness—
('And God had given his share')—he was not too
platonic to disdain the favours of at least one servant-
girl (he was arrested, August 1787, on a warrant
In meditatione fugæ), nor too punctilious to make
love to 'a Lothian farmer's daughter, a very pretty
girl, whom I've almost persuaded to accompany
me to the West Country, should I ever return,'
etc., nor too philosophical not to regret his Jean,
and reflect (in this very letter to Gavin Hamilton)
that he'd never 'meet so delicious an armful again.'

In the long-run his magnanimity suffered a certain
change. The peasant at work scarce ever goes
wrong; but abroad and idle he is easily spoiled,
and soon. Edinburgh was a triumph for Burns; but
it was also a misfortune. It was a centre of con-
viviality—a city of clubs and talk and good-fellowship, a city of harlotry and high jinks, a city (above
all) of drink :—

> 'Whare couthy chiels at e'enin meet,
> Their bizzin craigs and mou's to weet:
> An' blythely gar auld Care gae by
> Wi' blinket and wi' bleering eye':—

a dangerous place for a peasant to be at large in,
especially a peasant of the conditions and the stamp
of Burns. He was young, he was buckishly given,
and he was—Burns. He had, as certain numbers
in *The Merry Muses* witness, an entirely admirable

talent of a kind much favoured by our liberal
ancestors. To hear him talk was ever a privilege;
while to hear him make such use as he might of
this peculiar capacity cannot but have constituted
an unique experience. After all, a gift's a gift, and
a man must use the gifts he has. No reasonable
being can question that Burns used this one of
his.[1]   In those days he could scarce be buckish
—or even popular—and do other.   Even in the
country, says Heron, in his loose yet lofty way, 'the

[1] This is noted neither in praise nor in dispraise. It is noted
to show that Burns was essentially a man of his time: as how,
peasant of genius that he was, could he be anything else? Our
fathers loved sculduddery, and Burns, who came from Carrick
—where, as Lockhart has remarked, the Vernacular was spoken
with peculiar gaiety and vigour—was the best gifted of them
all in this respect by virtue of his genius, his turn of mind,
his peasanthood, and his wonderful capacity for talk.   Josiah
Walker notes of Burns that his conversation was 'not more
licentious' than the conversation heard at the tables of the
great; Lockhart regrets that he can give but few of Burns's *mots*,
for the reason that the most of those preserved and handed down
were unquotable.   It was a trick of the time, and long after—(remember Colonel Newcome's indignant retreat before old Costigan)
—so that Lord Cork of *The Bumper Toast*, and Captain Morris at
Carlton House and Burns among the Crochallan Fencibles are
but expressions of the same fashion in humour, the same tendency
in the human mind to apprehend and rejoice in the farce of sex.
I do not know that Burns and M'Queen of Braxfield (Stevenson's
Weir of Hermiston) ever met.   But it was said of M'Queen that
he had never read anything but sculduddery and law; and to
Ramsay of Auchtertyre, in whom Sir Walter found some elements
of Monkbarns, the two men seemed cast in the same mould.
Burns, in any case, was a man of the later Eighteenth Century
(he sent one of his best-known *facetiæ* to Graham of Fintry, with
a view to correcting some illiberal report about his politics); and to
take him out of it, and essay to make him a smug, decent, Late-
Victorian journalist is, as I think, to essay a task at once dis-
creditable in aim and impossible of execution.

votaries of intemperate joys, with persons to whom
he was recommended by licentious wit . . . had
begun to fasten on him, and to seduce him to em-
bellish the gross pleasures of their looser hours with
the charms of his wit and fancy.' These temptations
—(he was known, be it remembered, for the ribald of
The Fornicator and *The Court of Equity* as well as for
the poet of the *Mountain Daisy* and the *Saturday
Night*)—he was by no means incapable of putting by.
Mr. Arthur Bruce, indeed, 'a gentleman of great
worth and discernment,' assured Heron that he had
'seen the Poet steadily resist such solicitations and
allurements to convivial enjoyment, as scarcely any
other person could have withstood.' But—thus this
author : intelligent, not unfriendly on the whole, on
the whole competent—'the bucks of Edinburgh ac-
complished . . . that in which the boors of Ayrshire[1]
had failed. After residing some months in Edinburgh
he began to estrange himself, not altogether, but in
some measure, from the society of his graver friends.
. . . He *suffered* himself to be surrounded by a race of
miserable beings who were proud to tell that they
had been in company with Burns, and had seen
Burns as loose and as foolish as themselves.'[2] One
result of this condescension was this : always the

---

[1] This appears to be a polite description, by a staunch (though
drunken) Churchman, of those desperate spirits, Gavin Hamilton
and Robert Aiken.

[2] I give all this for what it is worth. Heron himself was something of a wastrel. Yet he had a clerical habit and a clerical
bias which made him easily censorious in the case of so hardened
and so militant an anti-cleric as the Bard. He was personally
acquainted, however, with that hero ; and his little biography
(1797) is neither unintelligent nor ill-written.

best man in the room, 'the cock of the company,' as Heron puts it, 'he began to contract something of new arrogance in conversation'; till in the long-run 'he could scarcely refrain from indulging in similar freedom and dictatorial decision of talk, even in the presence of persons [1] who could less patiently endure his presumption.' Heron's detail is vague—not to say indefinite; his effect may be misleading. But, as I said, the peasant at large—the peasant without hard work to keep him straight—must, almost of necessity, run to waste. And it is plain that, treading thus closely on the heels of 'the dissipation and riot,' the 'mason-meetings, drinking-matches, and other mischief,' of the year before, the distractions and the triumphs of Edinburgh continued the work which the mistakes and follies of Dumfries were to finish ten years after.

At last, however, the First Edinburgh Edition appeared (21st April 1787). The issue ran to 2800 copies, and 1500 of these were subscribed in advance. What Burns got for it is matter of doubt. Creech informed Heron that it was £1100—which is a plain untruth; Chambers says £500; Burns himself told Mrs. Dunlop (25th March 1789) that he expected to clear some £440 to £450. (Other impressions were called for in the course of the year, but the Bard had sold his copyright, and had no interest in them.) Whatever the amount,[2] Creech

---

[1] Heron himself, no doubt. He 'had the tongues,' and thought himself the better man.

[2] At the instancing of Henry Mackenzie, Creech paid Burns (23rd April 1787) a hundred guineas for the copyright of the *Poems*, besides subscribing five hundred copies. The Caledonian Hunt subscribed another hundred; and Burns sent seventy to

was a slow paymaster; and, as Edinburgh was bad
for Burns, and Creech was responsible for Burns's
detention in Edinburgh, it is impossible not to regret
that Burns had not another publisher. Burns in effect,
his Second Edition once published, had nothing to
do but pocket his receipts,[1] and be gone. This,

Ballantine for 'a proper person' in Ayr, and wrote from Dunse
(17th May) to acknowledge the receipt, from Pattison, the Paisley
bookseller, of 'Twenty-two pounds, seven shillings sterling,
payment in full, after carriage deducted for ninety copies' more.
Twenty-four copies went to the Earl and Countess of Glencairn,
twenty to Prentice of Conington Mains, forty to Muir of Kilmarnock, twenty-one to Her Grace of Gordon, forty-two to the Earl
of Eglintoun, and a certain number to the Scots Benedictionaries
at Maryborough and Ratisbon, and the Scots Colleges at Douay,
Paris, and Valladolid. The subscription price was five, the price
to non-subscribers six, shillings: the extra shilling being (Burns
to Pattison, *ut sup.*) 'Creech's profit.'

[1] Heron 'had reason to believe that he had consumed a much
larger proportion of these gains than prudence could approve;
while he superintended the impression, paid his court to his
patrons, and wasted the full payment of the subscription money.'
In effect, it is hard to see how, coming to Edinburgh with next to
nothing in his pocket (the £20 from Wilson could not have gone
very far), he could otherwise have lived. It would have been
natural enough for him to have accepted gratuities, for the Age
of Patronage was still afoot, and relief in this kind would have
come as easily (to say the least) to the 'ploughing poet,'
howbeit he was the proudest and in some respects the most
punctilious of men, as to any other. I find it hard to believe
that there were none. But there is no record of any; and a
letter (unpublished) of this period in acknowledgment of a gift
of money from Mrs. Dunlop is almost painful in its embarrassment of gratitude and discomfort. On the whole, I take it that,
however cheaply he lived in Edinburgh, he must of necessity have
had to discount his profits, though not to anything like the extent
suggested by Heron. Moreover, it is like enough that he spent a
certain amount upon his Tours, and it is certain that Mossgiel was
a dead loss to him.

however, was what Creech could not let him do: so that he went and came, and came and went, and it was not until the March of 1789 that the two men squared accounts.[1]

The Edition floated, comes a jaunt to the Border (begun 5th May) with Robert Ainslie. Then, by the 9th June, Burns is back at Mauchline, a much richer and a vastly more important person than he left it: able to lend his brother £180; reconciled, too, with Jean and her people, but disgusted, or feigning himself disgusted (for, after the repudiation, he is ever the superior and the injured party in regard to Jean), with the 'mean, servile compliance' with which his advances are met. Follows a tour to the West Highlands, which seems to be largely an occasion for drink and talk; and in July you find him back at Mauchline, boasting how he, 'an old hawk at the sport,' has brought 'a certain lady'—(unknown)—'from her aerial towerings, pop, down at my foot, like Corporal Trim's hat': despite which Jean is presently with child by him for the second time. In August he is at Edinburgh, intent on a settlement with Creech, but on the 25th he starts for the Highland tour with his friend Nicol.[2] After a couple of excursions more—

---

[1] Of the work he did about this time the best is to be found in the *Haggis* and the *Epistles* to Creech and the Guidwife of Wauchope House. What is very much more to the purpose is that he made Johnson's acquaintance, and at once began contributing to the *Musical Museum*.

[2] Heron describes Nicol as a man who 'in vigour of intellect, and in wild yet generous impetuosity of passion, remarkably resembled . . . Burns'; who 'by the most unwearied and extraordinary professional toil, in the midst of as persevering dissipa-

one to Ayrshire, to look at certain holdings—he is
resolved on quitting Edinburgh, settlement or no
settlement, to farm or go to the Indies, as circumstances shall dictate.   But it is written that his
life shall have another disputable episode and the
world an immortal scrap of song :—

> ' Had we never loved sae kindly,
>   Had we never loved sae blindly,
>   Never met or never parted,
>   We had ne'er been broken-hearted.'

So in the beginning of December he falls in with
Mrs. M'Lehose; he instantly proposes to ' cultivate
her friendship with the enthusiasm of religion';
and the two are languishing in Arcady in the
twinkling of a cupid's wing.

She was a handsome, womanly creature—' of a
somewhat voluptuous style of beauty': a style the
Bard appreciated—lively but devout, extremely sentimental yet inexorably dutiful: a grass widow with
children—nine times in ten a lasting safeguard—

---

tion . . . won and accumulated an honourable and sufficient
competence'; and who died of 'a jaundice, with a complication
of other complaints, the effects of long-continued intemperance.'
Burns admired Nicol, named a son after him, and immortalised
him as the 'Willie' who 'brew'd a peck o' maut.' He had a
generous heart and a brutal temper, with plenty of brains, a great
contempt for custom and the Kirk, and what Lockhart calls 'a
rapturous admiration of Burns's genius.' The violent vulgarity
of his behaviour at Castle Gordon is typical of the man. He
bought a little property not far from Ellisland, and, what with
pride and vanity and republican independence (so called) and an
immitigable turn for liquor, was certainly as bad a neighbour as
the Bard could possibly have had.

and the strictest notions of propriety—a good enough
defence for a time; but young (she was the Bard's
own age), clever, 'of a poetical fabric of mind,' and
all the rest. The upsetting of a hackney coach dis-
abled Burns from calling on her for some weeks.
But he wrote her letters, and she answered them; and
he was Sylvander, and she signed herself Clarinda;
and they addressed each other in verse as well as
prose; and she said it could never be; and he said
that at least he must know her heart was his; and
Religion was her 'balm in every woe'; and he gave
her his ideas of Deity; and, when they could meet,
Clarinda was ever afraid lest she had let Sylvander
go too far; and Sylvander, for his part, was monstrous
eloquent about 'Almighty Love'—(he was sometimes dreadfully like his favourite Man of Feeling)
—and was 'ready to hang himself' about 'a young
Edinburgh widow.' Widow she was not; but her
husband, who cared not a snap of the fingers for
her, was away in the West Indies; and it may
perhaps have suited her lover—who never, so far
as is known, was trained to the compromises and
the obsequiencies of adultery—to soothe his con-
science by making believe that the affair was at
the most a simple everyday amour. Clarinda was
of another make. In the prime of life, deserted,
sentimental, a tangle of simple instincts and as
simple pieties, she had the natural woman's desire
for a lover and the religious woman's resolve to
keep that lover's passion within bounds. It is
scarce questioned that she succeeded: though there
is a legend that a certain gallant and insinuating
little lyric:—

'O May, thy morn was ne'er sae sweet
As the mirk night o' December,
For sparkling was the rosy wine,
And secret was the chamber!
And dear was she I winna name
But I will aye remember!'—

commemorates, not only their final meeting (December 6th, 1791) but also, the triumph of the
Bard.[1] In any event she was plainly an excellent
creature, bent on keeping herself honest and her
lover straight; and it is impossible to read her
letters to Sylvander without a respect, a certain
admiration even, which have never been awakened
yet by the study of Sylvander's letters to her. For
Sylvander's point of view, as M'Lehose was still
alive, and an open intrigue with a married woman
would have been ruin, only one inference is possible: that he longed for the shepherd's hour to
strike for the chime's sake only; so that, when
he thought of his future, as he must have done
anxiously and often, he cannot ever have thought

---

[1] Both *Ae Fond Kiss* and *O May, thy Morn* were sent to
Clarinda after the final parting; but the legend is all-too obviously
an effect of the very common human sentiment in deference
to which so many novels end happily. For the rest, Sir Walter
Scott wrote thus on the fly-leaf of a copy of the very scarce
Belfast Edition (1806) of the *Letters Addressed to Clarinda
by Robert Burns*, now at Abbotsford:—'Clarinda was a Mrs.
Meiklehose, wife of a person in the West Indies, from whom she
lived separate but without any blemish, I believe, on her reputation. I don't wonder that the Bard changed her "thrice
unhappy name" for the classical sound of Clarinda. She was a
relative of my friend the late Lord Craig, at whose house I have
seen her, old, charmless and *devote*. There was no scandal at-
tached to her philandering with the Bard, though the Lady ran
risques, for Burns was anything but platonic in his amours,' etc.

of it as Clarinda's, even though in a moment of peculiar exaltation he swore to keep single till that wretch, the wicked husband, died.[1]

Very early in 1788, Jean—brought, she also, some time in the preceding summer 'pop, down at my feet, like Corporal Trim's hat'—was expelled her parents' house and took refuge at Tarbolton Mill. There Burns found her on his return, and thence he removed her to a house in 'Mauchline toun,' to the particular joy, a short while after, of Saunders Tait:—

> 'The wives they up their coats did kilt,
> And through the streets so clean did stilt,
> Some at the door fell wi' a pelt
>   Maist broke their leg,
> To see the Hen, poor wanton jilt!
>   Lay her fourth egg.'[2]

Follows what is perhaps the most perplexing sequence of circumstances in a perplexing life. To Clarinda, who knew of the affair with Armour, pitied

---

[1] M'Lehose outlived him many years.

[2] Some stanzas later in B—rns's *Hen Clockin in Mauchline*, Saunders (who has been likening Jean to a ship) thus notes her state:—
> 'Now she is sailing in the Downs,
> Calls at the ports of finest towns,
> *To buy bed hangings and galloons*':
and comments with fury on the fact that she's got, not only 'twa packs o' human leather,' but also
> 'A fine cap and peacock feather,
> And wi't she's douce,
> With a grand besom made of heather,
> To sweep her house.'
It is worth noting that he winds up his lampoon by accusing the gossips at the lying-in of talking scandal of the rankest and reading *The Holy Fair*!

the victim—(this does *not* mean that she wished
her married to Burns)—and had sped her shepherd
on his homeward way with 'twa wee sarkies' for the
victim's little boy: a mistress, be it remembered,
to whom he had written (14th February) in such
terms as these:—'I admire you, I love you as a
woman beyond any one in the circle of creation':
—he wrote, a few days after his arrival at Mauchline, that he had 'this morning' (23rd February
1788) 'called for a certain woman,' and been 'disgusted with her,' so that he could not 'endure her.'
Though his heart 'smote him for the profanity,'
he sought to compare the two; and ''twas setting
the expiring glimmer of a farthing taper beside the
cloudless glory of the meridian sun.' 'Here,' the
Old Hawk continues, '*here* was tasteless insipidity,
vulgarity of soul, and mercenary fawning. *There*,
polished good sense, Heaven-born genius, and the
most generous, the most delicate, the most tender
passion.' This to the contrary, it needs no great
knowledge of life, and still less of Burns and Armour,
to divine what happened; and it needs as little
of Burns at this point in his career to see why
he ended his confession to Clarinda thus:—'I
have done with her, and she with me.' Eight
days after this (3rd March 1788), in a letter to
Ainslie, some parts of it too 'curious' for a Victorian
page, he tells a different story.[1] 'Jean,' says he,

---

[1] The letter is best described as a Crochallanism—as something
written by one Fencible for the edification of another Fencible,
and dealing with its subject in right Fencible style and from the
correct Fencible point of view. I am afraid that, like the aforesaid letter to Clarinda, it was designed as what Ainslie himself,
then unregenerate, might have called 'a d——d bite.'

'I found banished like a martyr—forlorn, destitute, and friendless; all for the good old cause. I have reconciled her to her fate: I have reconciled her to her mother:[1] I have taken her a room: I have taken her to my arms: I have given her a mahogany bed: I have given her a guinea; and I have '—but here Scott Douglas's garbling begins, and Burns's inditing ends; and the original must be read, or the reader will never wholly understand what manner of man the writer was. Then comes an avowal so disconcerting that I cannot choose but disbelieve it, and conclude that it was made for some special purpose. 'But,' says the Old Hawk, 'but, as I always am, on every occasion—I have been prudent and cautious to an astounding degree; I swore her, privately and solemnly, never to attempt any claim on me as a husband, even though anybody should persuade her she had such a claim, which she had not,[2] neither during my life nor after my death. She did all this like a good girl, and . . .' The rest is unquotable. At first consideration, the spectacle of the Bard keeping 'the wish'd, the trysted hour,' with a settled purpose of 'prudence and caution' in his mind, and as it were the materials for swearing in his pocket, in no wise makes for enlightenment. On reflection, however, it becomes evident that Burns wrote thus to Ainslie, whom he had asked to call on Clarinda in his absence, simply that Ainslie might quote her his report of a second (and an entirely superfluous) act of

[1] Was reconciliation possible without a second offer of marriage? I doubt it.
[2] This is literally true: the 'unlucky paper' was destroyed.

repudiation on Jean's part : [1] to the end, as I cannot
doubt, of using the fact for all it was worth, when
he himself appeared upon the scene. That this is
at least a possible theory is shown by the terms in
which he tells (7th March) the story of his reconciliation to Brown : [2]—'I found Jean with her cargo
very well laid in. . . . I have turned her into a
convenient harbour where she may lie snug till she
unload, and have taken the command myself, not
ostensibly, but for a time in secret.' This can only
mean that he purposes to marry the girl. For all
that, though, he still has hopes of a practical issue to
his Edinburgh affair ; for in his next letter (writ the
same day) to Clarinda, who has reproached him for
silence, and at the same time owned that she counts
'all things (Heaven excepted) but lost, that I may
win and keep you,' ' Was it not blasphemy, then,'
he asks, 'against your own charms and against my
feelings, to suppose that a short fortnight could
abate my passion !' With a vast deal more to the
same purpose. Three days after, he starts again for
Edinburgh, and plunges deeper in desire than ever
for his 'dearest angel' (so he calls her on the
17th March), the 'dearest partner of his soul' (four
days after). 'Oh Clarinda' (same date), 'what
do I owe to Heaven for blessing me with such

---

[1] There was no need of oaths from Jean : her lover had had
his bachelor's certificate in his pocket for months. And such
swearing as there was—*was it not all on the other side ?*

[2] It is important to note the difference in manner and tone and
suggestion between Burns to Brown and Burns to Ainslie. Burns
writes to Brown as friend to friend ; to Ainslie as Fencible to
Fencible—much, in fact, as Swiveller, President of the Glorious
Apollos, to Chuckster, Vice of the same sublime Society.

a piece of exalted excellence as you!' He must
leave for Ellisland, *viâ* Mauchline, on the 24th; and
'Will you open,' he asks, 'with satisfaction and
delight a letter'—('twas all to be limited to letters
soon)—'from a man who loves, who has loved you,
and who will love you to death, through death, and
for ever!' They are to meet the next night, and
he is to watch—(right Arcady, this!)—her lighted
window :—' 'Tis the star that guides me to Paradise.'
And for him ' the great relish to all is—that Honor
—that Innocence—that Religion, are the witnesses
and guarantees of our happiness.' Follows a bit of
the Bible adapted to their peculiar case ; and with
an ' Adieu, Clarinda! I am going to remember you
in my prayers,' the Old Hawk stoops to his perch
for the night. Nothing is known of the last engagement; but apparently the citadel remains inviolate,
for the leaguer is raised next day, and the besieger
draws off his forces by way of Glasgow. Thence he
writes to Brown (26th March) that 'these eight days'
he has been 'positively crazed.' And by the 7th
April he has made Jean Armour his wife.

An amazing-love story ? True. But that love-
story it was—that Burns was first and last enamoured
of the woman he made his wife—is shown, I think,
by the fact that to all intents and purposes he
married her twice over. As for Clarinda, well . . . !
Clarinda complicates and exhilarates the interest to
this extent at least: that if words mean anything,
and the Bard be judged by those he wrote, the
Bard, had Clarinda been indeed a widow, might at
a given moment have found himself incapable of
making Jean an honest woman. And had he

followed his fancy, not his heart? How had the two Arcadians fared? 'Tis for some future Chambers to divine and say.

VII

Meanwhile he had taken Ellisland, a farm in Dumfriesshire, of Miller of Dalswinton: with an allowance from his landlord, a worthy and generous man, of £300, for a new steading and outhouses. His marriage at last made formal and public (it seems to have been celebrated by Gavin Hamilton), on the 5th August 1788 the bride and bridegroom appeared before the Session, acknowledged its irregularity, demanded its 'solemn confirmation,' were sentenced to be rebuked, were 'solemnly engaged to adhere faithfully to one another as husband and wife all the days of their life,' and were finally 'absolved from any scandal' on the old account. But the new steading was long a-building. It was not till the 6th November that Burns and Jean set up their rest in Dumfriesshire; and even so, they had to go, not to their own farmhouse—(it was not ready for them till the August of 1789)—but, to a place called 'The Isle,' about a mile away from it. Burns had taken Ellisland on the advice of a friendly expert;[1]

---

[1] 'A lease was granted to the poetical farmer' (thus Heron, who knew the country) 'at the annual rent which his own friends declared that the due cultivation of his farm might easily enable him to pay.' But those friends, being Ayrshiremen, 'were little acquainted with the soil, with the manures, with the markets, with the dairies, with the modes of improvement in Dumfriesshire'; they had estimated his rental at Ayrshire rates; so that, 'contrary to his landlord's intention,' he must pay more for Ellisland than Ellisland was worth. According to the elder Cunningham, Ellisland was a poet's choice, not a farmer's.

but he had had his doubts about the wisdom of 'guid
auld Glen's' decision, and these were soon justified.
For a time, however, he stuck to his work like a
man : conversing much, it would seem, in his leisure
with his neighbour, Glenriddell, and others, whose
honoured guest he was, making and vamping songs,
paying some heed to national and local politics,
and finding time for letters not a few—among
them a long and elaborate criticism on some worthless verses by that crazy creature, Helen Maria
Williams.[1] But by the end of July 1789 he had
resolved to turn his holding into a dairy farm to be
run by Jean and his sisters, and to take up his
Gaugership[2] in earnest; and on the 10th of August,
some brief while after the completion of *The Kirk's
Alarm,* he learned from Graham of Fintry (whom he
had met, in 1787, at the Duke of Athole's, on his
Second Highland Tour) that he was appointed
Exciseman for that district of Dumfriesshire in
which Ellisland is situate. The work was hard,
for he had charge of ten parishes, and must
ride two hundred miles a week to get his duty

---

[1] Burns was not only a reader himself : he was over the cause
of reading in others. One of his occupations at Ellisland was the
foundation and the management of a book-club. He took tho
keenest interest in the work, was especially careful in selection,
and, according to Glenriddell, did whatever must be done himself.
Like his father, he believed in education ; and, like his father, ho
did his best to educate his kind by all the means which lay to
his hand. He held that the peasant could not but be the better
for good reading ; and he exerted himself to the utmost to give tho
peasant what seemed to him the best that could be had. That he
did so is as honourable a circumstance as is found in his career.

[2] By Glencairn's interest he had been appointed to a place in
the Excise as early as 1787.

done. But by the beginning of December, ' I have
found,' he writes, ' the Excise business go a great
deal smoother with me than I expected'; and that
he 'sometimes met the Muses,' as he jogged through
the Nithsdale hills, is shown by the fact that *The
Whistle*, the excellent verses on Captain Grose
(with whom he made acquaintance at Glenriddell's
table), and *Thou Ling'ring Star*, with *Willie Brew'd*,
that best of drinking-songs, and *The Five Carlines*
(a notable piece of mimicry, if no more), all belong to the period of his probation, and were all
written before the end of the year. Plainly, too,
he was an officer at once humane and vigilant : since,
while it is told of him that he could always wink
when staring would mean blank ruin to some old
unchartered alewife (say), his first year's 'decreet'
—his share, that is, of the fines imposed upon his
information—was worth some fifty or sixty pounds.
Exercise and the open air are held good for a man's
health; yet in the winter of 1789-90 this man
suffered cruelly from his old ailment. As for verse,
the *Elegy on Matthew Henderson* and *Tam o' Shanter*
(1790) seem a poor year's output for the poet of
those wonderful months at Mossgiel. But work for
Johnson was going steadily on ; so that the results
of these barren-looking times are in a sort the best
known of his titles to greatness and to fame. Thus
he strove, and faltered, and achieved till 1791, by
the beginning of which year he had realised that
Ellisland was impossible; that he could not afford
his rent, which (so he told Mrs. Dunlop) was raised
that year by £20, and must depend entirely on his
Excisemanship : when he asked for service in a port,

and, by Mrs. Dunlop's interest, was transferred to
'a vacant side-walk' in Dumfries town.   Thither,
his landlord setting no manner of impediment in his
way, and his crops and gear having been well and
profitably sold,[1] he removed himself in December,
and established his family in a little house in the
Wee Vennel.

'Tis a circumstance to note that, beginning at
Ellisland as the Burns of *Of A' the Airts*, some
time before the end he was the Burns of *Yestreen
I Had a Pint o' Wine*.[2]   That is, he married Jean
in the April of 1788, and some two years after
he got Anne Park with child.   Jean bore him
his second son (in wedlock) the 9th April 1791;
and Anne Park had been delivered of a daughter
by him ten days before (31st March).   Some say
that she died in childbed; some that she lived to
marry a soldier.   Nobody knows, and, apparently,
nobody cares, what became of her.   *She* was no
'white rose' (with a legend).   She was scarce a

---

[1] The standing crops were 'rouped' in the last week of August.
They realised 'a guinea an acre above the average.' But such
a riot of drunkenness was 'hardly ever seen in this country.'
See Burns to Sloan (Scott Douglas, v. 394) for details and for a
confession:—'You will easily guess how I enjoyed the scene; as
I was no farther over than you used to see me':—which take
you back to the Burns of *The Jolly Beggars*. The stock and
gear 'were not sold till August' (Scott Douglas, v. 392). 'We
did not come empty-handed to Dumfries,' Mrs. Burns told
M'Diarmid. 'The Ellisland sale was a very good one. A
cow in her first calf brought eighteen guineas, and the purchaser
never rued his bargain. Two other cows brought good prices.
They had been presented by Mrs. Dunlop of Dunlop.'

[2] I have read somewhere that the first quatrain—the flower of
the song—is old; but I cannot verify the description.

'passion flower';[1] and though the Bard himself
thought the ditty he made upon her one of his best,
the 'episode' in which she played a principal part
is not regarded with any special interest by his
biographers. She was a tavern waitress, and he
was the Bard; and she pleased him; and she lived,
or died—it matters not which; and there's an end
on't. The true interest consists, perhaps, in the
magnanimity of Jean, who, lying-in a few days
after the interloper, was somehow moved to receive
the interloper's child, and to suckle it with her
own. It is further to note that Anne Park is the
last of Burns's mistresses who has a name. That
she was not the last in fact you gather from
Currie;[2] but this one is innominate. So far as is

---

[1] Chambers declares that, if Jean had not been away in Ayrshire, there would have been no Elizabeth Burns: which is surely
the boldest apology for a husband's lapse, at the same time that
it is the frankest admission of this particular husband's inability
to cleave to his wife in absence, that has ever been offered to an
admiring world. Scott Douglas knocks it on the head, and shows
that Chambers's valour is greater than Chambers's sense of
history, by proving that neither in the June nor the July of 1790
could Jean have been away.

[2] He has been roundly and deservedly reproved for the manner
and the circumstances in which he published his report—(of an
'accidental complaint')—which, by the way, was started by
Heron. For another piece of scandal, whether published or not
I do not know—that at Dumfries the Bard walked openly with
harlots—it is, of course, entirely unauthenticated; and I here
refer to it but for the purpose of pointing out that, if it were
true, the fact of such familiarities, however horrifying to respectable Dumfries, would sit lightly enough both on Burns the
peasant and on Burns the poet of *The Jolly Beggars* and *My
Auntie Jean Held to the Shore*: that, if it were true, the memory
of Burns exchanging terms with the light-heels of the port were
simply one to set beside the memory of Burton rejoicing in the
watermen at the bridge-foot at Oxford.

known, the goddesses of the years to come, the
Chlorises and Marias and Jessies:—

> '"Tis sweeter for thee despairing
> Than aught in the world beside':—

are all platonic in practice, if not in idea. The
recipe for song-making was soon to be this:—'I put
myself in the regimen of adoring a fine woman,
and in proportion to the adorability of her charms,
in proportion you' — Thomson — 'are delighted
with my verses.' It was a mistake, so far as the
world is concerned. But Burns made it; and by
the time it was made, he probably knew no better.
In his last years, indeed, the irresponsible Faunus
of Mossgiel and Edinburgh becomes a kind of
sentimental sultan, who changes, or rewards, his
slaves of dream with a magnificence which, edi-
fying or not, is at least amusing. Thus, you find
him designing the publication of a book of songs,
with portraits of the beauties by whom they are
inspired; Maria Riddell is expelled his lyrical
harem as with a fork, because she has offended
him; Jean Lorimer, she of 'the lint-white locks'
—('Bonie lassie, artless lassie!')—is the Chloris
of ditty after ditty, till of a sudden Chloris is a
disgusting name, and 'what you once mentioned
of "flaxen locks" is just'—so just, indeed, that
'they cannot enter into an elegant description
of beauty.'[1] This he discovers in the February

---

[1] Is it not all the Peasant and his womankind? The
peasant's women are his equals. The sentiment of chivalry is not
included in his heritage; and he treats his associates in that lot
of penury and toil which is his birthright as the 'predominant
partner,' the breadwinner, the provider of children, may: he

of 1796, in the July of which year he dies. And
he keeps up his trick of throwing the lyric hand-
kerchief till the end. All through his last illness
he is tenderly solicitous about his wife, be it remembered; yet the deathbed songs for Jessie
Lewars are the best of those closing years.

In the result, then, Ellisland was a mistake :
not so much because it was a farm, as because
it was not Burns's own.[1] He was essentially and
unalterably a peasant; and as a peasant-poet, a
crofter taking down the best verses ever dictated
by the Vernacular Muse, he might, one would like
to think, what with work in the fields, and work at
his desk, and the strong, persuasive inducements
of home, have attained to length of days and peace
of mind and the achievement of still greater fame,
at the same time that he realised the ideal which
he has sublimated in some famous lines :—

> 'To mak' a happy fireside clime
>   For weans and wife,
> That's the true pathos and sublime
>   Of human life.'

Plainly, though, it could not be. He had too much
genius, too much temperament, for it to be : with
too much interest in life, which to him, however
diverse and however variable his moods, meant,

---

punishes, that is, and he rewards. It is unlikely that this was
Burns's practice with Jean; but assuredly it was his practice
with the 'fine women' of his dreams.

[1] He would have liked the life well enough, he says, had he
tilled his own acres. But to take care of another man's, at
the cost, too, of a horrible and ever-recurring charge called rent—
that was the devil !

largely, if not wholly, Wine and Woman and Song.
Also, he had been too hardly used, too desperately
driven in his youth, and too splendidly petted and
pampered in his manhood, to endure with constancy
the work by which the tenant-farmer has to earn
his bread. He had seen his father fail at Mount
Oliphant and Lochlie; and he had shared his
brother's failure at Mossgiel. By no fault of his
own, but owing to the circumstance that he had
taken a holding out of which he could not make
his rent, he failed himself at Ellisland; and though,
in his case, there was small risk of 'a factor's snash,'
he was infinitely too honest and too proud to take un-
due advantage of another man's bounty : so, to make
ends meet, he turned gauger, and took charge of
ten parishes, and rode two hundred miles a week in
all weathers. It was a thing he'd always wanted
to do, and, at the time he took to doing it, it was
the only thing that could profitably be done by
him. But his misfortune in having to do it was
none the less for that. It took him from his home,
it unsettled his better habits, it threw him back
on Edinburgh and his triumphing experience as
an idler and a Bard, it led him into temptation
by divers ways. And when Pan, his goat-foot
father—Pan, whom he featured so closely, in his
great gift of merriment, his joy in life, his puissant
appetites, his innate and never-failing humanity
—would whistle on him from the thicket, he
could not often stop his ears to the call. He was
the most brilliant and the most popular figure in
the district; he loved good-fellowship; he needed
applause; he rejoiced in the proof of his own

pre-eminence in talk—rejoiced, too, in the tran-
scendentalising effect of liquor upon the talker,[1] as
in the positive result of his name and fame, his
prestance and his personality, upon adoring women.
Is it not plain that Dumfries was inevitable? Or,
rather, is it not plain that, first and last, the life
was one logical, irrefragable sequence of preparations for the death? That Mount Oliphant and
Lochlie led irresistibly to Mauchline, as Mauchline
to Edinburgh, and Edinburgh to Ellisland, and
Ellisland to the house in the Mill Vennel? And
is not the lesson of it all that there is none so unfortunate as the misplaced Titan—the man too great
for his circumstances? Speaking broadly, I can
call none to mind who, in strength and genius and
temperament, presents so close a general likeness
to Burns as Mirabeau. Born a noble, and given an
opportunity commensurate with himself, Burns would
certainly have done such work as Mirabeau's, and
done it at least as well. Born a Scots peasant,
Mirabeau must, as certainly, have lived the life and
died the death of Burns. In truth, it is only the
fortune of war that we remember the one by his
conduct of the Revolution, which called his highest
capacities into action, while we turn to the other for
his verses, which are the outcome (so Maria Riddell
thought, and was not alone in thinking) of by no
means his strongest gift.

---

[1] He complained (to Clarinda) long ere this of the 'savage
hospitality' he could not choose but accept. And, in effect, he
had the ill-luck to start drinking at a time when whisky, fire-
new from the Highlands, was the fashionable tipple, and was fast
superseding ale. Born a generation earlier, when ale and claret
were the staple comforters, he had stood a better chance.

VIII

Whatever the sequel, it may fairly be said for Ellisland that Burns and Jean were happy there, and that it saw the birth of *Tam o' Shanter* and the perfecting, in the contributions to Johnson's *Museum*, of the Vernacular Song.[1] The last, as we know, was Burns's work; but he had assistants, and they did him yeoman service. He worked in song exactly as he worked in satire and the rest—on familiar, old-established bases; but he did so to a very much greater extent than in satire and the rest, and with a great deal more of help and inspiration from without. I have said that he contributed nothing to Vernacular Poetry except himself, but, his contribution apart, was purely Scots-Traditional; and this is especially true of his treatment of the Vernacular Song. What he found ready to his hand was, in brief, his country's lyric life. Scotland had had singers before him; and they, nameless now and forgotten save as factors in the sum of his achievement, had sung of life and the experiences of life, the tragedy of death and defeat, the farce and the romance of sex, the rapture and the fun of

---

[1] I say nothing of the numbers sent to Thomson. Very many are copied from the *Museum*, and the others need not here be discussed with even an approach to particularity. A point to note in connexion with the contributions both to the *Museum* and to *Scottish Airs* is that Burns was honourably and intensely proud of them. He regarded them as work done in the service of the Scotland whose 'own inspirèd Bard' he was, and neither asked money, nor would take it, for them. To think that he was writing for Thomson to the very end is to have at least one pleasant memory of Dumfries.

battle and drink, with sincerity always, and often, very often, with rich or rich-rank humour. Among them they had observed and realised a little world of circumstance and character; among them they had developed the folk-song, had fixed its type, had cast it into the rhythms which best fitted its aspirations, had equipped it with all manner of situations and refrains, and, above all, had possessed it of a great number of true and taking lyrical ideas. Any one who has tried to write a song will agree with me, when I say that a lyrical idea—by which I mean a rhythm, a burden, and a drift—once found, the song writes itself. It writes itself easily or with difficulty, it writes itself well or ill; but in the end it writes itself. In this matter of lyrical ideas Burns was fortunate beyond any of Apollo's sons. He had no need to quest for them: there they lay ready to his hand, and he had but to work his will with them. That they were there explains the wonderful variety of his humours, his effects, and his themes: that he could live and work up to so many among them is proof positive and enduring of the apprehensiveness of his humanity, his gift of right, far-ranging sympathy. It is certain that, had he not been, they had long since passed out of practical life into the Chelsea Hospital of some antiquarian publication. But it is also certain that, had they not been there for him to take and despoil and use, he would not have been — he could not have been—the master-lyrist we know. What he found was of quite extraordinary worth to him; what he added was himself, and his addition made the life of his find perennial. But,

much as are the touch of genius and the stamp
of art, they are not everything. The best of many
nameless singers lives in Burns's songs; but that
Burns lives so intense a lyric life is largely due
to the fact that he took to himself, and made his
own, the lyrical experience, the lyrical longing, the
lyrical invention, the lyrical possibilities of many
nameless singers. He was the last and the greatest
of them all; but he could not have been the greatest by so very much as he seems, had these innominates not been, nor could his songs have been so
far-wandered as they are, nor so long-lived as they
must be, had these innominates not lived their lyric
life before him. In other terms, the atmosphere,
the style, the tone, the realistic method and design,[1]
with much of the material and the humanity, of
Burns's songs are inherited. Again and again his
forefathers find him in lyrical ideas, in whose absence
there must certainly—there cannot but have been—

---

[1] As I have said (see *ante*, pp. 278-9, Note 1), realism is the distinguishing note of the Vernacular School; and the folk-singers
are not less curious in detail than their literary associates and
forebears. Even that long sob of pain, *O, Waly, Waly*, has its
elements of everyday life and circumstance:—

> 'My love was clad in the black velvet,
>   And I myself in cramasie':—

its references to St. Anton's Well and Arthur's Seat and the
sheets that 'sall ne'er be pressed by me.' *Cf.*, too, that wonderful little achievement in romance, *The Twa Corbies*:—

> 'Ye'll sit on his white hause-bane,
>   And I'll pyke out his bonie blue een,
>   Wi' ae lock o' his gowden hair
>   We'll theek our nest when it grows bare.'

Cf., too, in other styles, *Toddlin Hame* and *Ellibanks and Elli-
bracs* and—well, any folk-song you care to try!

a blank in his work.   They are his best models, and
he does not always surpass them, as he is sometimes
not even their equal.[1]   And if his effect along
certain lines and in certain specified directions be
so intense and enduring as it is, the reason is that
they are a hundred strong behind him, and that he
has selected from each and all of them that which
was lyrical and incorruptible.   A peasant like themselves, he knew them as none else could ever know.
He sympathised from within with their ambitions,
their fancies, their ideals, their derisions, even as he
was master, and something more, of their methods.
And, while it is fair to say that what is best in
them is sublimated and glorified by him, it is also
fair to say that, but for them, he could never have
approved himself the most exquisite artist in folk-
song the world has seen.

It has been complained that, thus much of his
claim to be original removed, he must henceforth
shine in the lyrical heaven with a certain loss of
magnitude and his splendour something dimmed.
And this is so far true that the Burns of fact differs,
and differs considerably and at many points, from

---

[1] Cf. *O, Waly, Waly* and *The Twa Corbies* and *Helen of
Kirkconnel*; with *Toddlin Hame*, which Burns thought 'the first
bottle-song in the world,' the old sets of *A Cock-Laird Fu' Cadgie*
and *Fee Him, Father*, and, in yet another *genre*, *O, Were My Love*.
Even in *The Merry Muses* Burns, who wrote a particular class of
song with admirable gust and spirit, does no better work than
some of the innominates—the poets of *Erroch Brae* and *Johnie
Scott* and *Jenny M'Craw*, for example; while his redaction of
Ellibanks and Ellibraes—('an old free-spoken song which cele-
brates this locality would be enough in itself to bring the poet
twenty miles out of his way to see it')—is in no wise superior to
the original.

the Burns of legend. The one is an effect of certain long-lived, inexorable causes; the other—that 'formidable rival of the Almighty,' who, deriving from nobody, and appearing from nowhere, does in ten years the work of half-a-dozen centuries—is an impossible superstition, as it were a Scottish Mumbo-Jumbo. The one comes, naturally and inevitably, at the time appointed, to an appointed end; but by no conceivable operation in the accomplishing of human destiny could the other have so much as begun to be. And, after all, however poignant the regret, and however wide-eyed and resentful the amazement of those who esteem a man's work on the same terms as they would a spider's, and value it in proportion as it does, or does not, come out of his own belly, enough remains to Burns to keep him easily first in the first flight of singers in the Vernacular, and to secure him, outside the Vernacular, the fame of an unique artist. I have said that, as I believe, his genius was at once imitative and emulous; and, so far as the Vernacular Song is concerned, to turn the pages of our Third Volume is to see that, speaking broadly, his function was not origination but treatment, and that in treatment it is that the finer qualities of his endowment are best expressed and displayed. His measures are high-handed enough; but they are mostly justified.[1] He never boggles at appropriation,[2]

---

[1] Not always. See Vol. iii. (p. 96 and Note) for an attempt to improve upon Ayton (or another), and *ante* (p. 42 and Note) for another to improve upon Carew. Both are failures; but only one is in the Vernacular, and neither owns a Vernacular original.

[2] Besides the folk-singers and the nameless lyrists of the song-books, he is found pilfering from Sedley, Garrick, Lloyd,

so that some of his songs are the oddest conceivable mixture of Burns, Burns's original, and somebody Burns has pillaged.   Take, for instance, that arch and fresh and charming thing, *For the Sake of Somebody*.   In the first place, 'Somebody' comes to Burns as a Jacobite catchword ; and in the next, the lyrical idea is found in a poor enough botch by Allan Ramsay :—

> 'For the sake of Somebody,
> For the sake of Somebody,
>   I could wake a winter's night
> For the sake of Somebody.'

This is pretty certainly older than *The Tea-Table Miscellany*, and has nothing whatever to do with the verses which the later minstrel has tagged it withal. But it is a right lyrical idea, and in the long-run a lyrical idea is a song.   So thinks Burns ; and you have but to compare the two sets to see the difference between master and journeyman at a glance. The old, squalid, huckstering little comedy of courtship :—

> 'First we'll buckle, then we'll tell,
>   Let her flyte and syne come to . . .
> I'll slip hame and wash my feet,
>   An' steal on linens fair and clean,
> Syne at the trysting place we'll meet,
>   To do but what my dame has done ':—

Ramsay, Fergusson, Theobald, Carew, Mayne, Dodsley, and Sir Robert Ayton (or another). See also our Notes (Vol. iii.) on *Duncan Davison*, on *Landlady*, *Count the Lawin*, on *Sweetest May*, on *The Winter it is Past*, on *We're A' Noddin*, to name but these ; and, as a further illustration of his method, note that, according to Scott Douglas (MS. annotation), the first three lines of *Gat Ye Me* belong to old song No. i., the next five to Burns, and the last eight to old song No. ii.

gives place to a thing to-day as comfortable to the
ear and as telling to the heart as when Burns vamped
it from Ramsay's vamp from somebody unknown.
What is further to note is that not all the latest
vamp is Burns *plus* Ramsay *plus* Innominate I. *plus*
Jacobite catchword : inasmuch as the first line of
Stanza II. is conveyed from an owlish lover in *The
Tea-Table Miscellany* :—

'Ye powers that preside over virtuous love.'

Thus some solemn poetaster a good half-century at
least ere Burns; and for over a hundred years
'Ye powers that smile on virtuous love' has lived
as pure Burns, and as pure Burns is now passed
into the language.   Yet, despite the pilferings and
the hints, it were as idle to pretend that *Somebody*,
as it stands, is not Burns, as it were foolish to assert
that Burns would have written *Somebody* without a
certain unknown ancestor.   Another flash of illustration comes from *It Was A' For Our Rightfu' King*: with
its third stanza lifted clean from *Mally Stewart*, and
set in a jewel of Burnsian gold, especially contrived
and chased to set it off and make the lyric best of
it.   A third example is found in *A Red, Red Rose*,
which, as we have shown (iii. 143 and Note), is a
mosaic of rather beggarly scraps of English verse :
just as Jonson's peerless *Drink To Me Only With
Thine Eyes* is a mosaic contrived in scraps of
conceited Greek prose.   It is exquisitely done, of
course; but, the beggarly scraps of verse away,
could it ever have been done at all?   And *Auld
Lang Syne*?   It passes for pure Burns; but was the
phrase itself—the phrase which by his time had

rooted itself in the very vitals of the Vernacular—
was the phrase itself, I say, not priceless to him?
Something or nothing may be due to Ramsay for
his telling demonstration of the way in which it
should *not* be used as a refrain.   But what of that
older maker and the line which Burns himself
thought worth repeating, and which the world rejoices, and will long rejoice, to repeat with Burns :—

> *'Should auld acquaintance be forgot,*
>   An' never thocht upon ? '

Is there nothing of his cadence, no taste of his
sentiment, no smack of his lyrical idea, no memory
(to say the least) of his burden :—

> 'On old long syne, my jo,
>   On old long syne,
> That thou canst never once reflect
>   On old long syne' :—

in the later masterpiece?   To say ' No ' were surely
to betray criticism.   And *Ay Waukin, O*—should
we, could we ever, have had it, had there been
nobody but Burns to start the tune and invent the
lyrical idea ?

> ' O, wat, wat,
>   O, wat and weary !
> Sleep I can get nane
>   For thinkin o' my dearie.

> ' A' the night I wake,
>   A' the day I weary,
> Sleep I can get nane
>   For thinkin o' my dearie.'

Thus, it may be, some broken man, in hiding among
the wet hags; some moss-trooper, drenched and

prowling, with a shirtful of sore bones ! Whoever
he was, and whatever his calling and condition, he
had at least one lyrical impulse, he has his part in a
masterpiece by Burns, and his part is no small one.
I might multiply examples, and pile Pelion upon
Ossa of proof. But to do so were simply to repeat
the *Bibliographical* and the *Notes* to our Third
Volume; and in this place I shall be better employed
in pointing out that these double conceptions (so to
speak), these achievements in lyrical collaboration,
are for the most part the best known and the best
liked of Burns's songs, and are, moreover, those
among Burns's songs which show Burns the song-
smith at his finest. The truth is that he wrote two
lyric styles: (1) the style of the Eighteenth Century Song-Books,[1] which is a bad one, and in which

---

[1] He was trained in it from the first. In early youth he carried
an English song-book about with him—wore it in his breeches-
pocket, so to speak. This was *The Lark* : 'Containing a Collection of above Four Hundred and Seventy Celebrated English and
Scotch Songs, None of which are contain'd in the other Collections of the same size, call'd *The Syren* and *The Nightingale*.
With a Curious and Copious Alphabetical Glossary for Explain-
ing the *Scotch* words. London. Printed (1740) for John Osborn
at the Golden Ball in Pater Noster Row.' 'Tis a fat little book,
and as multifarious a collection of Restoration and—especially—
post-Restoration songs as one could wish to have. Antiquated
political squibs; ballads, as *Chevy Chace*, with *Gilderoy*, the
Queen's Old Soldier, and *Katherine Hayes*; a number of in-
decencies from D'Urfey's *Pills*; Scots folk-songs, like *Toddlin
Hame* and *The Ewe Bughts*, and *O, Waly, Waly* and *John
Ochiltree* and *The Blithesome Bridal*; current English ditties like
Old Sir Simon and *Phillida Flouts Me*; a song of a Begging
Soldier, whose vaunt, 'With my rags upon my bum,' is echoed in
The Jolly Beggars; much Allan Ramsay; with scattered examples
of Dryden, Dorset, Congreve, Alexander Scott, Brome, Prior,
Wycherley, Rochester, Farquhar, Cibber—even Skelton; and a

he could be as vulgar, or as frigid, or as tame, as very
much smaller men; [1] and (2) the style of the Vernacular Folk-Song, which he handled with that understanding and that mastery of means and ends which
stamp the artist. To consider his experiments in
the first is to scrape acquaintance with *Clarinda,
Mistress of My Soul,* and *Turn Again, Thou Fair
Eliza,* and *On A Bank of Flowers,* and *Sensibility,
How Charming,* and *Castle Gordon,* and *A Big-Bellied
Bottle,* and *Strathallan's Lament,* and *Raving Winds
Around Her Blowing,* and *How Pleasant the Banks,*
and *A Rosebud By My Early Walk,*[2] and many a thing
besides, which, were it not known for the work of a

wilderness of commonplace ditties about love and drink. On
the whole, an interesting collection. Particularly if you take it
as an element in the education of the lyric Burns.

[1] Cf. *Their Groves of Sweet Myrtle* (Vol. iii. 252-3 and Note),
among other things :—

> 'The slave's spicy forests and gold-bubbling fountains
>   The brave Caledonian views wi' disdain ;
> He wanders as free as the winds of his mountains,
>   Save Love's *willing fetters*—the chains o' his Jean.

Such achievements in what Mr. Meredith calls 'the Bathetic,' are
less infrequent in Burns than could be wished.

[2] It is understood that *Scots Wha Hae* is an essay in the
Vernacular (I gather, by the way, that it is one of the two or
three pieces by 'the Immortal Exciseman nurtured ayont the
Tweed' which are most popular in England). But, even so,
one has but to contrast it with *Is There for Honest Poverty,*
to recognise that in the one the writer's technical and lyrical
mastery is complete, while in the other it is merely academic—
academic as the lyrical and technical mastery of (say) *Rule
Britannia.* Now, *Is There for Honest Poverty* is *calqué* on
a certain disreputable folk-song ; while *Scots Wha Hae* is
for all practical purpose the work of an Eighteenth Century
Scotsman writing in English, and now and then propitiating the
fiery and watchful Genius of Caledonia by spelling a word as it
is spelt in the Vernacular.

great poet, would long since have gone down into
the limbo that gapes for would-be art.   In the
other are all the little masterpieces by which Burns
the lyrist is remembered.   He had a lead in *The
Silver Tassie* [1] and in *Auld Lang Syne*, in *A Man's a
Man* and *Duncan Davison*, in *A Waukrife Minnie*
and *Duncan Gray* and *Finlay*, in *I Hae a Wife* and
It Was A' For Our Rightfu' King and *A Red, Red
Rose*, in *Macpherson's Lament*, and *Ay Waukin, O,*
and *Somebody*, and *Whistle, and I'll Come to You*—
in all, or very nearly all, the numbers which make
his lyrical bequest as it were a little park apart—
an unique retreat of rocks and sylvan corners and
heathy spaces, with an abundance of wildings, and
here and there a hawthorn brake where, to a sound
of running water, the Eternal Shepherd tells his
tale—in the spacious and smiling demesne of
English literature.   And my contention—that it is
to Burns the artist in folk-song that we must turn
for thorough contentment—is proved to the hilt
by those lyrics in the Vernacular for which, so far
as we know, he found no hint elsewhere, and in
which, so far as we know, he expressed himself
and none besides.   He had no suggestions, it seems
(but I would not like to swear), no catchwords, no
lyrical material for *Tam Glen* and *Of A' the Airts*,
for *Willie Brewed* and *Bonie Doon*, for *Last May a
Braw Wooer* and *O, Wert Thou in the Cauld Blast*,[2]

---

[1] 'The first four lines are old,' he says, ' the rest is mine.'   And,
in effect, the quatrain is unique in his work.

[2] It is oddly and amusingly illustrative of Burns's trick of
mosaic that a line in this charming song .
        ' The brightest jewel in my crown ' :—
comes bodily from—*The Court of Equity* !

and *Mary Morison*—to name no more. But, if they
be directly referable to nobody but himself, they
feature his whole ancestry. They are folk-songs
writ by a peasant of genius, who was a rare and
special artist; and they show that the closer he
cleaved to folk-models, and the fuller and stronger
his possession by the folk-influence, the more of the
immortal Burns is there to-day.

Suggested or not, the songs of Burns were devised
and written by a peasant, devising and writing for
peasants. The emotions they deal withal are the
simplest, the most elemental, in the human list, and
are figured in a style so vivid and direct as to be
classic in its kind. Romance there is none in them,
for there was none in Burns [1]—'tis the sole point,
perhaps, at which he was out of touch with the
unrenowned generations whose flower and crown he
was. But of reality, which could best and soonest

---

[1] None, or so little that if his Jacobitisms seem romantic, it is
only by contrast with the realities in which they occur. The
interest of even *It Was A' For Our Rightfu' King* is centred in
the vamper's sympathy with, not the romantic situation :—

> ' He turned him richt and round about
> Upon the Irish shore,' *etc.* :—

but with that living, breathing, palpitating 'actuality' of sentiment developed in both hero and heroine by the disastrous turn
of circumstances :—

> ' Now a' is done that man can do,
> And a' is done in vain ' :—

and the position created by those circumstances at the end :—

> ' But I hae parted from my love
> Never to meet again ' :—

which places this lyric somewhere near the very top of homely
and familiar song.

bring them home to the class in which their genius
was developed, and to which themselves were
addressed :—

> ' Grain de musc qui gît invisible
> Au fond de leur éternité ' :—

there is enough to keep them sweet while the Vernacular is read. They are for all, or nearly all, the
peasant's trades and crafts : so that the gangrel
tinker shares them with the spinner at her wheel,
the soldier with the ploughman, the weaver with
the gardener and the tailor and the herd. Morals,
experiences, needs, love and liquor, the rejoicing
vigour and unrest of youth, the placid content
of age—there is scarce anything he can endure
which is not brilliantly, and (above all) sincerely
and veraciously, set forth in them. That old-world
Scotland, whose last and greatest expression was
Burns, either has passed or is fast passing away.
In language, manners, morals, ideals, religion, substance, capacity, the theory and practice of life—in
all these the country of Burns has changed : in some,
has changed ' beyond report, thought, or belief.' But
that much of her which was known to her Poet is
with us still, and is with us in these songs. For
man and woman change not, but endure for ever :
so that what was truly said a thousand years ago
comes home as truth to-day, and will go home as
truth when to-day is a thousand years behind. To
the making of these things there went the great
and generous humanity of Burns, with the humanity,
less great but still generous and sincere, of those
unknowns, whose namelessness was ever a regret to

him.[1] They are art in their kind. And there is
no reason why this 'little Valclusa fountain' should
lack pilgrims, or run dry, for centuries.[2]

IX

I purpose to deal with the Dumfries period with
all possible brevity. The story is a story of de-
cadence ; and, even if it were told in detail,
would tell us nothing of Burns that we have not
already heard or are not all-too well prepared to
learn. In a little town, where everybody's known

---

[1] 'Are you not quite vexed to think that these men of genius,
for such they certainly were, who composed our fine Scottish
lyrics, should be unknown?   It has given me many a heartache'
(R. B. to Thomson, 19th November 1794). And see his *Journal*
for a more heart-felt recognition still.

[2] They lived not long the limited life of Johnson's *Musical
Museum* and Thomson's *Scottish Airs*. Thus, in a collection of
North of England chap-books (c. 1810-20) which I owe to the kind-
ness of the Earl of Crawford, I find at least two Burns 'Songsters'
—(they are the same, but one is called 'The Ayrshire Bard's Song-
ster,' the other something else)—both 'Printed by J. Marshall in
the Old Fleshmarket,' Newcastle. In a third—a miscellany, this
one—is *Scots Wha Hae*, 'As sung by Mr. Braham at the Newcastle
Theatre Royal' (Carlyle thought this famous lyric should be 'sung
by the throat of the whirlwind'; but it had better luck than *that*).
The great Jew tenor further warbled a couple of stanzas of *The
Winter It is Past* at a concert in the same city, when Miss Stephens
was responsible for *Charlie He's My Darling*. In other chaps
Burns is found rubbing shoulders with Moore and Campbell and
Tom Dibdin, and a hundred others, among them Allan Ramsay.
In these *Of A' the Airts* is sandwiched between *The Twopenny
Postman* and the *Wedding at Ballyporcen*, while *Somebody* is
kept in countenance by *Paddy Carey* and *The Wounded Hussar*.
The most popular, perhaps, are *Of A' the Airts*, and *Scots Wha
Hae*, and *Willie Brew'd*; but *On a Bank of Flowers* lacks not
admirers.

to everybody, there is ever an infinite deal of
scandal; and Burns was too reckless and too con-
spicuous not to become a peculiar cock-shy for the
scandalmongers of Dumfries. In a little town,
especially if it be a kind of provincial centre, there
must of necessity be many people with not much to
do besides talking and drinking; and Burns was
ever too careless of consequences, as well as ever too
resolute to make the most of the fleeting hour—it
may be, too, was by this time too princely and too
habitual a boon-companion—to refrain from drink
and talk when drink and talk were to be had. In
the sequel, also, it would seem that that old jealousy
of his betters (to use the ancient phrase) had come
to be a more disturbing influence than it had ever
been before. He knew, none better, that, however
brilliantly the poet had succeeded, the man was
so far a failure as an investment, that, with bad
health and a growing family, he had nothing to look
forward to but promotion in the Excise; and his dis-
content with the practical outcome of his ambition
and the working result of his fame was certainly not
soothed, and may very well have been exacerbated,
by his rather noisy sympathy with the leading
principles of the French Revolution. He was too
fearless and too proud to dissemble that sympathy,
which was presently (1794) to find expression in one
of his most vigorous and telling lyrics; he was,
perhaps, too powerful a talker not to exaggerate its
quality and volume; and, though it was common,
in the beginning at least, to many Scotsmen, its
expression got him, as was inevitable, into trouble
with his superiors, and in the long-run was pretty

certainly intensified, to the point at which resentment
is translated into terms of indiscretion and imprudence, by the reflection, whether just or not,[1] that
it had damaged his chances of promotion. That
he fought against temptation is as plain as that
he proved incapable of triumph, and that, as Carlyle
has wisely and humanely noted, the best for him,
certain necessary conditions being impossible, was
to die. Syme,[2] who knew and loved him, said that he
was 'burnt to a cinder' ere Death took him; we can
see for ourselves that the Burns of the Kilmarnock
Volume and the good things in the *Museum* had

---

[1] It seems to have been unjust. Pitt, though he loved the
poetry of Burns, did nothing for him—was probably, indeed, too
busy to think of doing anything once the page was read and the
bottle done; and Fox, to whom Burns looked for advancement,
was ever out of office, and could do nothing, even had he been
minded to do something, which we are not told that he was.
But the Bard had a sure stay in Graham of Fintry; and, though
Glencairn was dead, and he was sometimes reprimanded (*et pour
cause*), there is no reason to believe that he would have missed
preferment had he lived to be open to it.

[2] It has been said, I believe, that Syme's evidence is worthless,
inasmuch as it tends to discredit Burns. But one eye-witness,
however dull and prejudiced (and Syme was neither one nor
other), is worth a wilderness of sentimental historians; and Syme's
phrase, howbeit it is so picturesque that it conveys what is,
perhaps, too violent an impression, probably means no more than
that Burns had damaged himself with drink. That much Burns
admitted time and again; and Currie—who cannot but have got
his information from Maxwell—remarks that for over a year
before the end 'there was an evident decline of our Poet's
personal appearance, and, though his appetite continued unim-
paired, he was himself sensible that his constitution was sinking.'
It was all, the doctor thought, the effect of alcohol on a difficult
digestion and a sensitive nervous system; and, though he was
something of a fanatic in this matter, I see no reason, as he was
also an honest man, to question his diagnosis.

ceased to be some time before the end; there is
evidence that some time before the end he was
neither a sober companion nor a self-respecting
husband. And the reflection is not to be put by,
that he left the world at the right moment for
himself and for his fame.

There is small doubt that the report of his mis-
conduct was at best unkindly framed; there is none
that certain among his apologists have gone a very
great deal too far in the opposite direction. We may
credit Findlater, for instance, but it is impossible,
having any knowledge of the man, to believe in the
kind of Exciseman-Saint of Gray: impeccable in all
the relations of life and never the worse for liquor:
even as it is impossible to believe in the *bourgeois*
Burns of the latest apotheosis. As Lockhart says,
the truth lies somewhere between the two extremes;
and one is glad to agree with Lockhart. Even so,
however, tradition, as reported by friends and enemies
alike, runs stronger in his disfavour than it does
the other way.[1] And, though we know that party
feeling ran high in Dumfries, and that Burns—
with his stiff neck, and his notable distinction,
and his absolute gift of speech—did certainly damn

---

[1] 'We are raising a subscription (horrid word)'—(thus Sir
Walter, to Morritt, 15th January 1814)—'for a monument to
Burns, an honour long delayed, perhaps till some parts of his
character were forgotten by those among whom he lived.' This
was written within twenty years of Burns's death: when the
grievance of the Revolution was lost in the shadow cast by the
tremendous presence of Napoleon. And, if it be urged that
Burns's offending against Toryism must have been rank indeed to
be recalled thus bitterly and thus late, it may be retorted that by
no possibility can it have been an hundredth part so indecent as

himself in the eyes of many by what, in the circumstances, must have seemed a suicidal intemperance of feeling and expression, we know also that, once extremely popular, he was presently cut by Dumfries society; that after a time his reputation was an indifferent one on other counts than politics; and that more than once—as in the case of Mrs. Riddell, and again, when he had to apologise for a toast no reasonable or well-bred man would have proposed in the presence of a King's officer, unless he were prepared to face the consequences— he behaved himself ill, according to the standard of good manners then and now. The explanation in these and other cases is that he was drunk; and, as matter of fact, drink and disappointment were pretty certainly responsible between them for the mingled squalor and gloom and pathos of the end. There is nothing like liquor to make a strong man vain of his strength and jealous of his prerogative—even while it is stealing both away; and there is nothing like disappointment to confirm such a man in a friendship for liquor. Last of all, there needs but little knowledge of character and life to see that to apologise for Burns is vain: that we must accept him frankly and without reserve for a peasant of genius perverted from his peasanthood, thrust into a place for which his peasanthood and his genius

---

the conduct of the Parliamentary Whigs during the life and long after the death of Pitt. Of all men living Burns was entitled to an opinion; of all men living he had the best gift of expression. Well, he had his opinion, and he used his gift; and Dumfries could not forgive him. It is again a question of circumstances. Fox and the rest were honoured Members of His Majesty's Opposition. Burns was only an exciseman.

alike unfitted him, denied a perfect opportunity, constrained to live his qualities into defects, and in the long-run beaten by a sterile and unnatural environment. We cannot make him other than he was, and, especially, we cannot make him a man of our own time : a man born tame and civil and unexcessive—'he that died o' Wednesday,' and had obituary notices in local prints. His elements are all-too gross, are all-too vigorous and turbulent for that. 'God have mercy on me,' he once wrote of himself, 'a poor damned, incautious, duped, unfortunate fool ! the . sport, the miserable victim of rebellious pride, hypochondriac imaginations, agonising sensibility and bedlam passions.' Plainly he knew himself as his apologists have never known him, nor will ever know.

That his intellectual and temperamental endowment was magnificent we know by the way in which he affected his contemporaries, and through the terms in which some of them—Robertson, Heron, Dugald Stewart, and, especially, Maria Riddell— recorded their impression of him ; yet we know also that, for all its magnificence, or, as I prefer to think, by reason of its magnificence, it could not save him from defeat and shame. Where was the lesion ? What was the secret of his fall? Lord Rosebery, as I believe, has hit the white in saying that he was 'great in his strength and great in his weaknesses.'[1] His master-qualities, this critic

---

[1] I note with pleasure that Lord Rosebery knows too much of life, and is too good a judge of evidence, to think of putting a new complexion on the facts of these last, unhappy years. But has he been explanatory enough? What, after all, but failure is possible for strength misplaced and misapplied ?

very justly notes, were 'inspiration and sympathy.'
But if I would add 'and character'—which, to be
sure, is largely an effect of conditions—how must
the commentary run? There is pride—the pride of
Lucifer : what did it spare him in the end ? There
is well-nigh the finest brain conceivable; yet is
there a certain curious intolerance of facts which
obliges the owner of that brain, being a Government
officer and seeing his sole future in promotion, to
flaunt a friendship with roaring Jacobins like Maxwell and Syme, and get himself nicknamed a 'Son
of Sedition,' and have it reported of him, rightly
or not, that he has publicly avowed disloyalty at
the local theatre.[1]   There is a passionate regard
for women; with, as Sir Walter noted, a lack of
chivalry which is attested by those lampoons on
living Mrs. Riddell and on dead Mrs. Oswald.
There is the strongest sense of fatherhood, with
the tenderest concern for 'weans and wife'; and
there is that resolve for pleasure which not even
these uplifting influences can check.   There is a
noble generosity of heart and temper; but there is
so imperfect a sense of conduct, so practical and so
habitual a faith in a certain theory :—

---

[1] I do not for an instant forget that here is more circumstance :
that he was a true Briton at heart, and that in the beginning his
Jacobinism was chiefly, if not solely, an effect of sympathy with
a tortured people.   But there are ways and ways of favouring an
unpopular cause; and Burns's were alike defiant and unwise.
Thus Maxwell was practically what most people then called a
'murderer'—of the French King; yet it was while, or soon after,
the enormities of the Terror were at their worst, that he became
a chief associate of Burns.   To some this seems a 'noble imprudence.'   Was it not rather pure incontinence of self ?

'The heart ay 's the part ay
That maks us richt or wrang ' :—

that in the end you have a broken reputation, and
death at seven or eight and thirty, is the effect of
a variety of discrediting causes. Taking the precisian's point of view, one might describe so extraordinary a blend of differences as a bad, well-
meaning man, and one might easily enough defend
the description. But the' precisian has naught to
do at this grave-side; and to most of us now it is
history that, while there was an infinite deal of the
best sort of good in Burns, the bad in him, being
largely compacted of such purely unessential defects
as arrogance, petulance, imprudence, and a turn for
self-indulgence, this last exasperated by the conditions in which his lot was cast, was not of the worst
kind after all. Yet the bad was bad enough
to wreck the good. The little foxes were many
and active and greedy enough to spoil a world
of grapes. The strength was great, but the weaknesses were greater ; for time and chance and
necessity were ever developing the weaknesses at
the same time that they were ever beating down
the strength. That is the sole conclusion possible.
And to the plea, that the story it rounds is very
pitiful, there is this victorious answer :—that the
Man had drunk his life to the lees, while the Poet
had fulfilled himself to the accomplishing of a
peculiar immortality ; so that to Burns Death came
as a deliverer and a friend.

W. E. H.

INDEX TO ESSAY

Printed by T. and A. CONSTABLE, Printers to Her Majesty
at the Edinburgh University Press

OPINIONS OF THE PRESS
On Mr. Henley's Essay in *The Centenary Burns.*

THE TIMES.
Interesting, brilliant, full of original things.

SCOTSMAN.
There have been many more or less remarkable literary portraits of the 'poet and peasant,' but nothing so worthy of attentive study as Mr. Henley's essay has been published since the *Edinburgh Review* passed judgment upon Lockhart's *Life*. . . . Fine as his essay is as a piece of literary history and criticism, it is not less so, rather more so, in its summing up of the life of Burns. Certainly he extenuates nothing ; but that is not what he is there for. There have been more sins of this kind done by writers about Burns than can ever be covered by the affectation of charity ; and it takes good-will and more to make so true a portraiture as his. To seek a comparison from the art of painting, the work is like a picture by Meissonier, so accurate in detail, so much in little space, pathetic and serene. Every word of it is well felt and well written . . . and Mr. Henley's essay will always be profitable reading for those who desire a knowledge of the poet's art and the man's character.

ATHENÆUM.
The crowning feature of the volume is, of course, Mr. Henley's essay on the poet and the man. Of the

i

man—the typical 'peasant of genius perverted from his peasanthood, thrust into a place for which his peasant-hood and his genius alike unfitted him, denied a perfect opportunity, constrained to live his qualities into defects, and in the long-run beaten by a sterile and unnatural environment'—our essayist's estimate is more just than that of those who dream of a 'tame, proper, figmentary Burns,' and more favourable than the colder apprecia-tion of others who cannot quite forgive the peasantly limitations, even in consideration of the essential gran-deur of Mr. Henley's 'inspired faun.' . . . Mr. Henley believes strongly that Jean from first to last was her husband's real love, will have none of Mary Campbell, and damns the fancy for Clarinda with the epithet Arcadian — on the whole, an estimate which, however each one may modify it for himself, is sane, consistent, and generous. Burns's best friends believed that his poetry was not the biggest part of him. But for the world that is his abiding monument. And hereof Mr. Henley discourses in masterly fashion.

SPEAKER.

An essay which is one of the finest pieces of English, one of the sanest and soundest pieces of criticism, one of the most vivid and remarkable portraits our time has known.

GLASGOW RECORD.

It is not possible to follow Mr. Henley further in his thoughtful, eminently critical, and finely suggestive essay ; but alike in individuality of style and freshness of treatment it is worthy to bear comparison with the famous essay of Carlyle, while the poet in the author gives him a fuller equipment than had even Carlyle for the task. The result is an essay which will at once be recognised as of the elect in literature, and which would have given distinction to an edition less entitled to it on other grounds than is the *Centenary*.

ii

GLASGOW MAIL.

There has been too much headlong, irreflective, and ill-formed eulogism in the past, and we frankly admit that Mr. Henley's roughly expressed common-sense views in regard to Burns come to us with bracing freshness after the gush and the sentiment that seem to have inspired every one of his editors but Lockhart.

ACADEMY.

We hold that in plan, scope, and judgment this is proper biography. The day of the Pious Editors, who would reconcile everything to their piety, is over. We need the lives of men as they lived them—up, down, and straight through—where their lives touched their work, and where their work influenced their contemporaries. Such a life as that set down here : Burns himself—not another.

ACADEMY.

In conclusion, let us hope that Mr. Henley's courage and sincerity will purify the atmosphere about Burns. As in the case of the Chinese Emperor's clothes, one has spoken, and now many may begin to speak. But, as in Andersen's story, to say that first word it needed, if not a child, what is in some ways the same—a man of genius.

SATURDAY REVIEW.

Mr. Henley has written nothing better than this essay, nothing more vivid and elastic in style, nothing in a more masculine temper, nothing that touches with a more competent freshness a hackneyed theme. Nothing could be better than the way in which Mr. Henley indicates what the effect of the rough life at Mount Oliphant must have been upon the boy. On Mrs. M'Lehose and Mrs. Dunlop he is delightful, and he treats the whole 'old Hawk' business exactly as it deserves, neither too seriously nor with too much levity. At every turn he lightens the tissue of his disquisition by some phrase or flash of suggestive description which delights the attention. What could be better, for instance, than the little vignette of the wild snatch of song murmured by 'some broken man, in hiding among the wet hags; some moss-trooper, drenched and prowling, with a shirtful of sore bones'? His treatment of Burns's love-adventures is as excellent in one way as the editors' treatment of his text is in another.

BORDER ADVERTISER.

The best part of the volume, however, comes at the last in the shape of the essay by Mr. Henley, which, with an index thereto, occupies the remaining 118 pages. So much has been said and written about Burns that the essayist's task was certainly not an easy one, as everybody is familiar with all the facts of the poet's life. He has succeeded, however, in attaining his object, writing succinctly and naturally, making no attempt to hide Burns's faults, while he gives due credit to his genius. It is an able attempt to indicate the connection between Burns's life and Burns's poetry, to define his relation to the men of his own time and the past, to pourtray his circumstances and surroundings, and to illustrate and analyse the special character of his achievement in verse.

PERTHSHIRE ADVERTISER.

Mr. Henley at the close of the volume gives a scholarly narrative, with appropriate comments, of the poet's life. This narrative may be taken as an accurate review of the poet's life, and will be widely read ' ecause of the labour and research that have been bestowed upon it.

BIRMINGHAM POST.

The essay is throughout penetrating, manly, outspoken, and pictures for us the real Burns as man and poet.

iv

DAILY CHRONICLE.

It must not be understood that Burns, or any rational Burnsite, has, in our opinion, just cause of complaint against Mr. Henley. On the contrary, no critic has treated the man with more sympathy (for the mere idealising whitewasher cannot be said to be in. 'sympathy' with his subject) or has shown a warmer appreciation of the poet. The mischief is that Mr. Henley's zeal is zeal with knowledge, and to zeal without knowledge nothing can be more offensive. It cannot be expected that any one man's estimate of a character, in many ways so baffling as that of Burns, will ever absolutely hold the field. On this point, Mr. Henley has spoken with sense, insight, and good feeling, but he has not said the last word. As to Burns's artistic ancestry, on the other hand, and his place in Scottish literature, we think that Mr. Henley has left little more to be said. His conclusions may be modified in detail—we ourselves would sometimes phrase them differently — but in substance and effect they cannot be overthrown.

PALL MALL GAZETTE.

Those who admire and love Burns with intelligence will welcome this essay as the most comprehensive, critical, and incisive, and as therefore the most appreciative and just, that has yet been published on the greatest poet that Scotland has produced. . . . But it is impossible to compress Mr. Henley. His essay on Burns must be read in its entirety if you are to appreciate the insight, the breadth of view, the unerring accuracy of stroke that distinguish the last and best essay on the genius and achievement of Robert Burns.

ST. JAMES'S GAZETTE.

None but an idolater could complain of his treatment of Burns in this very remarkable summing-up of his work and genius : ' He came of the people on both sides ; he

z   v

had a high courage, a proud heart, a daring mind, a matchless gift of speech, an abundance of humour and wit and fire ; he was a poet in whom were quintessentialised the elements of the Vernacular Genius, in whose work the effects and the traditions of the Vernacular School, which had struggled back into being in the Kirk's despite, were repeated with surpassing brilliancy ; and in the matter of the Kirk he did for the people a piece of service equal and similar to that which was done on other lines and in other spheres by Hutcheson and Hume and Adam Smith.'

STANDARD.

Mr. Henley's eagerly anticipated 'terminal essay' on the 'Life and Genius of Burns' is a well-balanced and artistic example of literary portraiture. It is written in full and unflinching view of all the facts, and no attempt is made either to hide or to extenuate moral weakness. Robert Burns is too great a man, and his achievements are too commanding, to call for the services of trumpery apologists. Mr. Henley has, therefore, done well to rescue the personal character of Robert Burns from the adulation of his hysterical admirers. His method of treatment seems to us at once more honest and more wholesome, and there is the resistless force of truth in the sane and final verdict.

PUBLISHERS' CIRCULAR.

The essay is an exceedingly fine piece of writing, critical in the best sense, and in every way worthy of its subject and its writer.

STAR.

One turns with eager interest to Mr. Henley's promised essay on the 'Life, Genius, and Achievement' of the poet. One finishes it with the satisfaction that Burns has at last found his true editor and critic. . . . Of Burns the man Mr. Henley's is the first fearlessly human reading.

vi

LEEDS MERCURY.

It is quite clear that in undertaking his part as editor of this Centenary Edition Mr. Henley felt that he had a mission. The real Burns was in danger of passing into oblivion, giving place to an utter mortal, more resem-bling, we learn, a journalist of the later Victorian era than a Scottish peasant of the last century. In the judgment of Mr. Henley Burns has suffered so many things at the hands of his editors that it was high time some one, not only with the necessary knowledge, but with the still more necessary courage, should come forward and reveal to the world the man as he really lived and talked among his fellows, and to estimate at its proper value the genius of the poet. That is what Mr. Henley has set himself to do, more especially in the essay which forms the fitting climax to his Centenary Edition. Henceforward they are without excuse who do not know what manner of man Robert Burns was from the cradle to the grave.

MANCHESTER GUARDIAN.

The completion of the Centenary Edition of Burns by Messrs. T. C. and E. C. Jack has given Mr. W. E. Henley, who edits it in conjunction with Mr. T. F. Henderson, an opportunity of contributing a most strik-ing essay upon the character and genius of the Scottish poet. In a recent criticism of Mr. Henley, surprise was expressed that a man who knew so much about Burns should not himself be a Scotchman. An element of thankfulness will in future mingle with such sur-prise, for while, since Carlyle's famous essay, no such valuable criticism of Burns's work as that now offered has been produced, it may be said that never has Burns's character and its relations to his work been more power-fully and frankly set forth.

THE WORLD.

This final division of a work which places all lovers of Burns under a heavy obligation to everybody concerned in its production is rendered additionally interesting by the inclusion of a critical appreciation of the peasant-poet's character, career, and achievement, from the pen of Mr. Henley, whose keen and judicially plain-spoken analysis is all the more welcome because it presents so striking a contrast to the essays in blindly apologetic hero-worship customary in similar circumstances. But if Mr. Henley 'nothing extenuates,' he assuredly 'sets down naught in malice,' and his luminous study of the influence which Burns's· in many respects unfortunate life exercised upon his work leaves no ground of legitimate complaint to the poet's most ardent admirer.

BIRMINGHAM GAZETTE.

In the masterly essay which closes Vol. iv. Mr. Henley has presented the poet as he was.

MANCHESTER COURIER.

Since Carlyle's famous essay, no such valuable criticism of Burns's work as that now offered has been produced : it may be said that never before has Burns's character and its relation to his work been more powerfully and frankly set forth.